STACEY AND THE
STOLEN HEARTS

**Other books by
Ann M. Martin**

Leo the Magnificat
Rachel Parker, Kindergarten Show-off
Eleven Kids, One Summer
Ma and Pa Dracula
Yours Turly, Shirley
Ten Kids, No Pets
Slam Book
Just a Summer Romance
Missing Since Monday
With You and Without You
Me and Katie (the Pest)
Stage Fright
Inside Out
Bummer Summer

THE KIDS IN MS. COLMAN'S CLASS series
BABY-SITTERS LITTLE SISTER series
THE BABY-SITTERS CLUB mysteries
THE BABY-SITTERS CLUB series
CALIFORNIA DIARIES series

STACEY AND THE STOLEN HEARTS

Ann M. Martin

AN
APPLE
PAPERBACK

SCHOLASTIC INC.
New York Toronto London Auckland Sydney

No part of this publication may be reproduced in whole or in part, or stored in a retrieval system, or transmitted in any form or by any means, electronic, mechanical, photocopying, recording, or otherwise, without written permission of the publisher. For information regarding permission, write to Scholastic Inc., Attention: Permissions Department, 555 Broadway, New York, NY 10012.

ISBN 0-590-05973-4

12 11 10 9 8 7 6 5 4 3 2 1   8 9/9 0 1/0 2/0

Printed in the U.S.A.   40
First Scholastic printing, February 1998

The author gratefully acknowledges
Ellen Miles
for her help in
preparing this manuscript.

CHAPTER 1

Ever been around when an asteroid slammed into the Earth, destroying everything in its path and creating total chaos?

No?

I haven't either. But I think I could handle an asteroid attack, now that I've been through another type of natural disaster.

Valentine's Day.

I'll never understand it. It's supposed to be a pleasant little romantic holiday. Why does it usually end up causing trouble and heartache instead?

I sat back in my seat. I was on a train headed for New York City to spend the rest of Valentine's Day with my boyfriend, Ethan. And I thought about the Valentine's Day that will go down in history, the one I'd just survived.

But before I tell you all about it, let me introduce myself. My name's Stacey — Anastasia Elizabeth McGill, if you want to be formal. I'm an only child, I'm thirteen years old, I'm in the eighth grade, and I live in Stoneybrook, Connecticut. More basic facts about *moi*? I'm tall, with blonde hair, which used to be long and permed, but recently I had it cut shoulder-length — I just needed a change. I do pretty well in school, especially in math, my favorite subject. I'm even on Stoneybrook Middle School's math team, the Mathletes. We recently became state champs!

You may think it's a little unusual for a thirteen-year-old to be taking the train to Manhattan by herself. Well, I suppose it might be for most thirteen-year-olds, but it's not for me. For one thing, I grew up in Manhattan, so I know the city like the back of my hand. (Have you ever thought about that expression? It's a little weird, isn't it? Who cares if you know the back of your hand?) I've always known how to hail a cab, choose the best restaurant for lunch, or find the coolest new boutique.

For another thing, I still visit Manhattan on a regular basis. To see Ethan? Well, yes, though I only met him recently. To check out Bloomingdale's, my favorite store? Absolutely. But really, there's one major reason I go to Manhattan: to see my dad.

My parents are divorced.

I live in Stoneybrook with my mom. Dad still lives in the city. I love them both, so you can

2

imagine how hard it was when they told me I had to pick where — and with whom — I wanted to live. Stoneybrook edged out the Big Apple, even though I'd only lived there for a little while. That was before the divorce, when my dad had been transferred here briefly. The main reason? The friends I'd made during that time. I'd joined this great club, the BSC (short for Baby-sitters Club), and I became instant Friends 4-Ever with each and every club member. But more about that later.

My parents' divorce was one of the two biggest things that ever happened to me. The other was finding out I have diabetes. If you know anyone with diabetes, you might understand what that means. If not, let me explain. Basically, there's an organ in your body called the pancreas, which is supposed to make a hormone called insulin, which helps regulate your blood sugar. Well, your pancreas may be doing its job, but mine sure isn't. So I have to help it out, by testing my blood sugar regularly, injecting myself with insulin every day (it sounds awful, but I'm used to it), and being careful about what I eat. I mean *very* careful. If I don't eat right, I can become extremely sick. (That's why I'd brought a snack — Wheat Thins and an apple — with me on the train. I knew it would be a long time before dinner.)

Oh, one other thing about diabetes. It's not

like a cold or the flu that makes you feel miserable for a little while and then you recover. It's a lifelong disease. Maybe I'll be lucky and someone will come up with a cure during my lifetime, but for now I have to take the long view and cope with it the best I can. Diabetes can make you feel different, apart from other people. I try not to let it do that. Even though I'm constantly aware of my health, even though I've been to more doctors than most people four times my age, even though I could get seriously ill eating a chocolate bar, I always try to remember that I'm more than just a diabetes patient. I'm a person who happens to have diabetes.

My friends are great about it. They're supportive and understanding and altogether cool. So's Ethan.

In fact, Ethan's amazing. It hasn't been long since we first met, yet I feel as if I've known him all my life. He's sweet and funny and caring, and I can talk with him about anything. We've had a few ups and downs but now we're definitely up. He also happens to rate about a gazillion on the hunk-o-meter: long, almost black hair, a tiny gold hoop in one ear . . . sigh.

But my relationship with Ethan goes way beyond caring how he looks. This thing with Ethan is different, new. I've gone out with plenty of boys. In fact, I have to admit (blush, blush) I even used to be a little boy-crazy. There was Toby, at Sea City, and Sam, my friend Kristy's older brother. There was Wes, the student teacher I had a Texas-sized crush on, and Pierre, my first boyfriend-on-skis. I went out briefly with Terry, a mysterious boy who lived in Stoneybrook only for a short time, and with RJ, one of the more popular boys at school, and with Pete, and with Ross.

And then there was Robert.

Robert Brewster was my first serious boy-friend, and I know I'll never forget him. He was on the basketball team when we first met, and I loved watching him play. Robert and I went out for quite awhile. It wasn't a perfect relationship, but we worked through the hard times. Then, not long ago, we broke up for good. I think the breakup was a long time coming, but that didn't make it any easier when it finally happened. I was hurt because he'd started seeing another girl, with whom I was sort of friendly, before we'd even broken up. Yuck.

That's all history now. I'm over Robert, and I imagine he's over Andi Gentile. (That's the girl he was seeing. She goes to SMS too.) Some-times I wonder, though. Lately I've seen Robert looking gloomy when I pass him in the halls at school. He used to be cheerful, always laugh-

5

ing and joking, but something's changed. We haven't talked much since our breakup, so I don't know what's going on with him.

Anyway, back to Ethan. He and I had planned a super-romantic time together in New York. We were going to have dinner at a cozy little French restaurant, then go for a carriage ride through Central Park (touristy, but definitely romantic). Finally, we'd go dancing. Ethan had promised to teach me how to tango!

After that, I planned to spend most of the weekend with my dad. On Sunday, I'd hop a train back to Stoneybrook.

Stoneybrook. Home of the Great Valentine's Day Disaster. As my train entered the tunnel that would bring us into Manhattan, I tried to remember how it had all started. I thought back to a BSC meeting a couple of weeks earlier and remembered that it was there that the subject of Valentine's Day had first come up.

CHAPTER 2

Okay, quick personality quiz. Valentine's Day is coming. You want to send a card to one of your best buds. Which type tickles your eyeballs when you stroll into your friendly neighborhood card shop?

A) Classic. Hearts and flowers rule.

B) Silly. The way to my heart is through my funny bone.

C) Artsy. I have elegant taste. No Garfield, please.

D) Cute. I've never met a puppy I didn't love.

Which did you pick? I lean toward the classic, myself. I'm a sucker for mushy poems and pictures of sunsets. Anyway, I do believe the kind of card you send says something about who you are. That's what I was thinking about as I looked around the room at my fellow BSC members. I was remembering last Valentine's Day, when I received cards from each and every one of them (we love to celebrate holidays). The cards they picked out were exactly what I would have expected. In fact, I probably could have matched cards to friends without even checking the signatures.

Take Kristy, for example. That's Kristy Thomas, the president of the BSC. Last year, she sent me a valentine with a picture of an old-time baseball player on it. Inside, it said, "I'd go to bat for you anytime."

Perfect. Kristy really is the kind of friend who'll stand by you, no matter what. Also, Kristy's a sports fiend, and baseball's probably her favorite game. She even coaches Kristy's Krushers, a softball team for little kids.

Kristy's always full of ideas and full of the energy it takes to see ideas through. In fact, the BSC was Kristy's idea. She saw how hard it often was for her mom to find a sitter for her younger brother and realized that parents would probably love knowing they could call one number and reach several responsible, caring sitters. She was right. As soon as we started the club the calls began to pour in.

We meet three times a week, on Mondays, Wednesdays, and Fridays from five-thirty until six. During those times parents can call us to set up sitting jobs. When they do, our secretary, Mary Anne Spier, who keeps track of all our schedules plus tons of client information, checks our club record book to see who is free for which jobs. Since there are seven of us (nine, when you count our associate members, who don't come to meetings but who fill in as necessary), we hardly ever have to say no to a parent. Not that we'd want to anyway. We love kids and we adore sitting for them, mainly because we make sure it's fun. The only thing that isn't much fun about sitting is writing up our jobs in the club notebook, a chore Kristy insists on. But I have to admit, you learn a lot when you read everybody else's entries, and parents love that we're always up-to-date on their kids. When we're on the job we don't just hang around raiding the fridge and channel surfing. Instead, we play games, read books out loud, organize special events, and generally have a great time with our charges. And, on those days when we feel less than inspired, or there's a need for extra inspiration, we bring along our Kid-Kits: boxes we've filled with hand-me-down toys and games, plus stickers and markers.

Kid-Kits were Kristy's idea too. She's determined to make the BSC a successful business. In fact, Kristy is Ms. Determination. I think she inherited her mother's drive. Kristy's mom raised four kids (Kristy; her younger brother,

David Michael; and her two older brothers, Charlie and Sam) on her own after her husband walked out on the family.

Now Kristy's mom is married again, this time to a really good guy. His name is Watson Brewer, and he came as a package deal. He has a cat, two kids (Karen, seven; and Andrew, four) from his first marriage, *their* pets, a mansion, and tons of money. A mansion? Tons of money? That's right. It just so happens that, besides being a good-natured, funny guy, Watson happens to be immensely rich. He has megamoney. (I have to say that if my mom ever decides to marry again, I wouldn't mind a stepdad like Watson. I'd have a charge card for every store in Manhattan!)

Watson's mansion is so huge that it doesn't seem crowded. Which is amazing, because the family has continued to grow since he and Kristy's mom married. First came Shannon, a Bernese mountain dog puppy. She's named after Shannon Kilbourne, who gave her to the Thomases. Shannon lives in Kristy's neighborhood, and she's one of our associate members. Then came Emily Michelle, an adorable toddler who was born in Vietnam and was an orphan until Watson and Kristy's mom adopted her. And the latest arrival is Nannie, Kristy's grandmother, who came to help out.

Full house? No kidding. But it's a happy

household, and Kristy seems to thrive on the chaos.

Her best friend, Mary Anne, the BSC's secretary, wouldn't last a day at the mansion. She's Kristy's total opposite: shy, quiet, and very private. They don't seem to have anything in common other than looks. Both of them are somewhat vertically challenged (short, in other words) and have brown hair and eyes. Still, they've been friends since they were in diapers.

Go figure, as a New Yorker would say.

Mary Anne's valentine to me last year? A card featuring a fluffy gray kitten (similar in looks to her kitten, Tigger) cuddling up to a teddy bear. Yes, Mary Anne goes for cute with a capital C. She likes romance too. In fact, she's had a steady boyfriend for quite awhile. His name's Logan Bruno and he's our other associate member. Whenever Logan does something romantic, Mary Anne is likely to burst into tears. Tears come easily to Mary Anne. I caught her crying once while we were watching a nature show. She couldn't stand how mean the animals were to each other.

Mary Anne's family is smaller but almost as complicated as Kristy's. For a long time, her family was tiny — just Mary Anne and her dad. Her mom died when Mary Anne was just a baby. Then her dad remarried . . . and the bride was his recently divorced high school

11

sweetheart (how romantic). Mary Anne gained a stepmother, a stepbrother, a stepsister, and a best friend. That's three people, not four. The stepsister, Dawn Schafer, was Mary Anne's friend, and a member of the BSC, even before the families blended.

Mary Anne was very happy about Richard, her dad, marrying Sharon, Dawn's mom. But she didn't have long to experience life in a bigger family. First Jeff, Dawn's younger brother, decided he'd rather live in California, where he and Dawn had grown up and where their father still lives. Then, after awhile, Dawn decided that she belonged on the West Coast too. That was hard on Mary Anne. She misses Dawn *muchissimo.* We all do.

Dawn is an honorary member of the BSC. When she was here, she was the BSC's alternate officer. That meant she could fill in for any other officer who wasn't able to make it to a meeting.

That job is now covered by Abby Stevenson, the BSC's newest member. Abby moved here recently from Long Island. She's a fellow New Yorker, though not a Manhattanite. I didn't receive a valentine from her last year, but I bet I will this year, and I'd bet all the money in the BSC treasury that it will be a funny one, the funniest one she can find. Abby has a wild sense of humor. You should see the imitations she does. And she's always cracking jokes and making puns.

Abby is an identical twin. Her sister's name is Anna, and though they look alike, with dark curly hair and dark eyes, they are different in most other ways. Abby loves sports and is a terrific athlete, despite the fact that she has allergies and asthma that keep her sniffling and sneezing, gasping and wheezing. Anna, on the other hand, loves music and plays her violin for hours a day. She hasn't let the fact that she has scoliosis (a slight — in her case — curvature of the spine, for which she wears a brace) slow her down.

Abby and Anna live near Kristy with their mom, who commutes to Manhattan for her job as an executive editor at a big publishing company. Their dad died several years ago in a car wreck. Neither of them talks about him much, but I know they miss him terribly. I'm no psychiatrist, but I have a feeling that Abby's love for joking and Anna's devotion to music may have something to do with how they're working through their dad's death.

Whew! Heavy. On a lighter note, let me introduce my best friend, Claudia Kishi, vicepresident of the BSC. I'll never forget the valentine she sent me last year, in part because I look at it every day. It was such a work of art that I had it framed and hung it on my wall.

Claudia would never dream of buying a valentine. She's an arts-and-crafts virtuoso, and nobody I know is more creative. Her valentine was an abstract painting in red, white, and gold. There were no cupids or hearts, but the feeling of love came shining through.

Our club meets in Claudia's room, mainly because she has her own phone with a private line, which is essential for our business. Hosting meetings is Claudia's main duty as vice-president. As far as I can tell, the job has no other official duties. Unofficially, Claudia is responsible for providing munchies for each meeting, a job she carries out with great pleasure. You see, she is the Junk Food Queen of the Universe. Workers in the Ring-Ding factory probably toil away beneath a gold-framed portrait of Claudia.

Her parents know nothing of her royal standing. They forbid her to eat junk food or, for that matter, to read what they consider junk literature, such as Nancy Drew mysteries. So her room is full of hiding places stuffed with bags of Chee-tos and boxes of Junior Mints, not to mention Nancy Drew mysteries. I should mention that Queen Claud is always kind enough to have sugar-free snacks, such as pretzels, on hand for me.

Somehow, Claudia's eating habits have had no impact on her looks. Her figure is trim and her skin is clear. Claudia, who is Japanese-American, is a knockout. She has long, straight black hair (always decorated with the accessory *du jour*) and dark, almond-shaped eyes. As you can imagine, her creative nature leads her to dress with incredible style. She may not be an awesome student like her older sister, Janine the Genius (in fact, Claud spent some time back in seventh grade this year), but she definitely has her own talents.

Speaking of talents, I should mention that my talent for math is what led me to take the job as the BSC treasurer. I am responsible for collecting dues every Monday and for keeping track of how much money we have in the treasury. We use the money for things such as Claudia's phone bill and Kristy's transportation costs. (Watson's mansion is across town, so Kristy's brother Charlie drives her and Abby to meetings. We pay for his gas.)

I received two other BSC valentines last year, from our junior officers, who are both eleven years old and in the sixth grade. (The rest of us are thirteen and in the eighth.) As junior officers, Jessi Ramsey and Mallory Pike aren't allowed to sit at night for anyone other than their own siblings, which means that they take many of our afternoon sitting jobs.

Jessi and Mal are best friends. They love horses (the card Mal sent me featured a white horse on a beach) and reading. Jessi's totally involved in ballet (her card had a dancer on it), while Mal spends a lot of time writing and drawing. She wants to be an author/illustrator of children's books someday. Mal is white, with reddish-brown hair and freckles, and she wears — and detests — glasses. Jessi's African-American, with deep brown eyes and strong, ballet-toned legs. Jessi has a younger sister, a baby brother, and an aunt who lives with the family. Mal has *seven* younger sisters and brothers. No wonder she's such a good sitter!

In fact, at that day's meeting, Mal's sisters and brothers were the main topic of conversation.

"They're driving me even more nuts than usual," Mal complained. "It's this Valentine's Day business."

We groaned.

"When did it become so competitive?" she asked. "I mean, they're all talking about how many cards they're going to receive, and who's sending the best ones, and which of them will be given candy or flowers. It's ridiculous!"

"You're right," agreed Kristy. "Kids that age shouldn't be worrying about Valentine's Day. It should just be a fun holiday." She stopped talking and her eyes took on a faraway look. I could tell she was in Idea Mode.

"My mom feels the same way," said Claudia.

16

"She's thinking of having some kind of party in the children's room." Claudia's mom is head librarian at the Stoneybrook Public Library.

"What a great idea," put in Jessi. "Becca is all caught up in Valentine's Day too. She'd love to have a party to go to." Becca is Jessi's eight-year-old sister.

"A festival!" said Kristy suddenly.

"Huh?" we replied.

"We'll combine forces with the staff of the children's room and throw a big Valentine's Day festival for all the kids. We can figure out the details later." Her eyes were gleaming. "What do you think?" she asked.

We thought it was a great idea. We also knew it didn't really matter what we thought. Kristy was on a roll, and the festival, which hadn't even existed until two seconds earlier, was on. This year's Valentine's Day was going to be a special one for the kids of Stoneybrook, and for their sitters.

CHAPTER 3

"Oh, I don't know, Pete. I mean, why me?"

Pete shrugged. "You're a natural," he said. "You've helped out with Pep Squad, you're a Mathlete, you helped organize the Mischief Night Masquerade." He smiled. "I know you can do it. And besides, it'll be fun."

I had to admit that Pete's idea did sound like fun. "Let me think about it," I said. "I'll give you an answer by the end of the day."

"Deal," Pete replied. "Fish sticks, please," he said to Mrs. Orr, one of the cafeteria workers at Stoneybrook Middle School. She smiled at Pete and loaded up his plate.

Pete Black, who is president of the eighth-grade class, had ambushed me while I stood in line in the cafeteria. Most days I bring my own lunch, but that day — the morning after our BSC meeting — I'd overslept and hadn't had time to throw together a sandwich.

I chose fish sticks too, even though they're

far from being a favorite food of mine. With their crunchy breaded coating, I knew they'd fulfill both the carbohydrate and protein servings for my midday meal. A container of milk, some salad, and an apple would round out my lunch.

I paid for my meal and carried my tray over to the BSC's usual table. Kristy and Mary Anne were already there, along with Claudia. (It's *great* to have her back at eighth-grade lunch.) Abby, who'd been behind me in line, was threading her way toward us through the crowded, noisy cafeteria. Just as she sat down, somebody near the trash cans dropped a tray, and the whole cafeteria burst into applause and whistles. We're such a mature bunch.

I knew Jessi and Mal (who eat lunch with the sixth-graders) would want to hear about Pete's idea, but I couldn't wait until our next BSC meeting to talk about it. "Listen to this, guys," I began as soon as Abby had pulled up a chair.

"Ew," interrupted Kristy. She was staring at my plate in horror.

I sighed and shook my head. "Yes?" I asked. "You have a problem with my lunch?" I should have known better.

"That's lunch?" Kristy was grinning wickedly. "I thought it was some failed project from woodshop." She leaned forward to take a closer look. "And are those gopher guts I see?"

she asked, pointing to the little cup of tartar sauce. "Yum," she said, raising her eyebrows and rubbing her stomach. "Sure wish I'd bought that instead of this boring old cheese sandwich." She held up a plain sandwich that featured a slice of yellow cheese between two slabs of white bread.

Her boring old sandwich looked pretty good all of a sudden. But I wasn't about to let her immature and totally gross comments about my food keep me from enjoying, or at least eating, my lunch. After all, I should be used to this routine by now. Kristy never lets a lunch period go by without giving us some disgusting commentary on what we're eating.

"Actually, it's monkey snot," I said calmly, dipping a fish stick into the tartar sauce. "Want to try some?" I held the fish stick in her direction.

"Ew! Ew!" cried Kristy. She jumped back in her seat and put up her hands in self-defense. Her face looked a little green.

Ha. I'd grossed out the gross-out queen.

I took a big bite of my fish stick and tried not to make a face. I knew it wasn't really made of wood shavings and glue, but it sure tasted as if it were. "Anyway," I said, "listen. I have big news about Valentine's Day."

Kristy groaned. "I'm already sick of Valentine's Day, and it's still weeks away," she said.

"I mean, I want to make it fun for the kids, but other than that I'd just as soon forget about it."

I gave her a sympathetic look. Valentine's Day can be a drag if there's nobody special in your life. Kristy used to have a sort-of boyfriend, Bart Taylor, but they barely speak now. I understood why she'd rather avoid the topic of Valentine's Day.

Claudia, on the other hand, looked eager to hear my news. She has a new boyfriend, a guy named Josh Rocker. He was one of her best seventh-grade friends, and he was secretly in love with her for ages. It must have been torture for him when she was going out with this other seventh-grader named Mark. But Josh stuck it out until Claudia finally realized that Mr. Rocker was her true Mr. Right. Ah, new love.

Mary Anne has no problem with Valentine's Day either. Why should she? She has Logan for a boyfriend, and Logan always comes through in the romance department.

And Abby? She's happily single.

As far as our younger friends' romantic lives, Jessi is kind of in the same category as Abby. And Mal sometimes goes out with a guy named Ben Hobart.

That's the BSC Romance Roundup. Now, back to that day in the cafeteria.

"Pete Black has this great idea," I told my

friends. "It's a fund-raiser for the eighth grade."

"So, what is it?" asked Kristy. She looked skeptical. She has always had a hard time believing that anyone else can come up with the kind of great ideas she's known for.

"Valentine-grams," I said. I sat back, crossed my arms, and smiled at my friends.

"Huh?" said Claudia.

"How do they work?" asked Mary Anne.

"They sound neat, whatever they are," said Abby.

"They sound dumb," said Guess Who.

"It's easy," I said, remembering how Pete had explained it to me. "We'll set up a table during the two weeks before Valentine's Day. People can fill out forms — valentine messages to send to friends or secret admirers. We'll charge a dollar per message."

"Not me," blurted Kristy.

I could tell she thought the idea was a good one, which was making her cranky.

I ignored her. "We'll collect the messages, sort them, and deliver them — along with a bag of candy hearts for each valentine-gram — on Valentine's Day. Simple, romantic, and very cool, no?"

"No," said Kristy.

But the others shouted her down. "It sounds terrific," said Abby.

"I love it," agreed Claudia. I could already imagine the "creative" spelling that would adorn her valentine-gram to Josh.

"It's so romantic," Mary Anne said. She looked a little teary-eyed.

"Personally, I think *anti*-valentine-grams would sell better," muttered Kristy. "I could send one to Cokie, for example."

We all looked across the lunchroom to the table where Cokie Mason, the person the BSC loves to hate (not really, but we *do* dislike her), has been sitting lately with her new boyfriend, Brent Jensen.

"It looks as if she and Brent might be sending *each other* anti-valentine-grams," murmured Claudia.

Sure enough, Cokie was glaring at Brent, and Brent was frowning at Cokie. They both looked seriously irked.

"Cupid has his work cut out for him there," whispered Mary Anne with a giggle.

We all cracked up.

Then I noticed Robert, and I stopped laughing. He was sitting at a table in the corner with his usual bunch of friends. But while his friends were clowning around the way they always do, he was just staring off into space, looking distracted and kind of sad. I also noticed Jacqui Grant, a girl I used to be friends with until I discovered that her middle name is

Trouble. *She* had definitely noticed Robert. In fact, she was gazing (that's the only word that really describes what she was doing) at him thoughtfully. Was she trying to decide whether or not to send him a valentine?

Speaking of which, I realized that I might as well let Pete know I'd be glad to help out. After all, it sounded like too much fun to pass up. I'd seen Pete leave the lunchroom a few minutes earlier, so I said good-bye to my friends, dumped the trash from my tray, and took off after him.

"Hey, McGill," I heard someone call as I left the lunchroom. I turned to see Cary Retlin standing by the water fountain, wearing his customary smirk.

Cary is new to SMS, but he's already gained quite a reputation. His main mission in life is causing trouble, mostly by pulling complex practical jokes. He's not the type to put whoopee cushions on people's chairs. He's much more subtle than that. Whoopee cushions are more Alan Gray's style. More about him later.

"Hi, Cary," I said. "Have you seen Pete Black?"

"He's on his way to gym," he answered. "I'm in the same class. Should I tell him you're on board for the valentine-gram project?"

My jaw dropped. How did he know? I was too shocked to do anything but nod.

"I think you'll have an exciting time with that," said Cary as he walked away.

Exciting? Fun, yes. Amusing, maybe. But what could make the valentine-gram project *exciting*? I looked at Cary as he ambled down the hall, and thought about the word he'd chosen. At that precise moment, I felt a little tingle go down my spine.

I didn't know it at the time, but that was definitely a premonition. Cary's prediction was about to come true.

CHAPTER 4

VALENTINE-GRAM

To: Claudia
From: ~~An~~ admirer
Sometimes roses are white
And sometimes violets are too
I've been as high as a kite
Ever since I first kissed you.

I sighed. I couldn't help myself. Josh looked up at me and blushed so hard that his face matched the red hearts decorating the table. "You read it?" he asked.

"Sorry!" I said. "I didn't mean to. It's just that your writing is so clear, and — I couldn't help —" I was babbling.

Josh interrupted me, waving a hand impatiently. "It's okay," he said. "The main thing is, do you think she'll like it? Or will she think it's lame? You're her best friend, right? You should know." He bit his lip and looked at me nervously.

"Are you kidding?" I asked. "Claudia will *love* it. Any girl would. It's the sweetest, most romantic —"

He interrupted me again, this time with a big sigh of relief. "Great. Thanks, Stacey! I'm late for class." He shoved the slip of paper toward me, along with a dollar.

After I'd said good-bye to Josh, I folded up his valentine-gram, stuck it into an envelope, sealed it, and addressed it to Claud. Then I added it to the growing stack inside the bag we were using to store and carry around the completed valentine-grams. (We also had an envelope to keep the money in, and a notebook for keeping track of who'd sent valentine-grams.)

This was my third day at the valentine-gram

table, and I'd been having the time of my life. I felt like one of Cupid's helpers. (Can't you just see me sporting designer wings and a bow and arrow?) I'd helped love-struck sixth-graders compose innocent notes. I'd seen seventh-grade girls giggle over the silliest poems. And I'd watched as one of the most popular boys in the eighth grade nervously scrawled out his deepest feelings for a girl he'd probably never even spoken to.

It was fascinating. And hilarious. And touching.

On the first day, Pete and I had set up the table just before sixth-grade lunch. We had special permission to miss a few classes, as long as we stayed caught up on our work. Our plan? To operate the booth through all three lunch periods every day, as well as before homeroom and after last period. Pete and I would take turns staffing the table, and at especially busy times we'd both be there. The eighth-grade class officers would help out when it was time to deliver the valentine-grams, but for now it was only Pete and me. I thought we'd just be handing out blank forms, loaning pens to kids who didn't have them, and collecting money, but the job turned out to be much more involved.

"How do you spell 'infatuated'?" asked Justin Price, a sixth-grader who was our first customer of the day. I knew he was in Mal's math class, and I wondered if he might have a secret crush on her. I helped him spell a few words: "passionate," "bewitched," "enchanted." This kid was serious about his valentine! When he finally finished, I couldn't resist peeking as he addressed the sealed envelope. "To Ms. Vandela," he wrote, and I had to fake a huge sneezing fit to cover up my giggles. Skinny little Justin had just written the love letter of all time to a teacher we call Dolly Two, after Dolly Parton. Ms. Vandela has the same big hair, big something-else, and heavy hand with the makeup as the star she's nicknamed after. Picturing her with Justin was almost more than I could bear.

Justin gave me a suspicious look as he slipped his completed valentine-gram into the Gap shopping bag I'd donated to the cause. As I watched him make his deposit, I realized the blue-and-white bag was going to be holding a lot of important messages by the end of the week.

Business was steady during that first day. Kids were coming to the table in twos and threes, filling out valentine-grams and slipping them into the bag. Some customers seemed nervous and wrote out their messages quickly, while others, who also seemed nervous, took forever to translate their thoughts to paper. Some kids were very, very careful to shield their writing from me, but others didn't seem to care. A lot of bad poetry flashed before my eyes that day.

Plenty of sixth- and seventh-graders sent valentine-grams, but business really heated up during the eighth-grade lunch period. I never knew so many of my classmates were die-hard romantics.

Take Alan Gray, otherwise known as the most obnoxious boy in the eighth grade, for example. He's always cracking jokes and acting like a dweeb. I'd never have thought he was capable of tender feelings. But there he was at the table, blushing and stammering and being very, very careful to hide what he was writing and who he was writing it to.

Or Cokie Mason. She's always seemed cold-hearted to me. (Example: She once tried to steal Logan away from Mary Anne. Enough said?) But Valentine's Day was melting the Ice Queen. She must have written and sent about five valentine-grams to Brent Jensen over those first three days, and that was only during my shifts at the table.

"So, has he sent me any?" she asked on the first day.

"Can't tell you," I answered. Pete and I had decided to keep who sent what to whom our secret.

She looked disappointed. "Well, if he hasn't, I'm sure he will."

On the second day, I noticed her hanging around the table, keeping an eye out for Brent. He didn't show up. "He's probably waiting until the last minute," she confided to me. "Isn't that just like a boy?"

On the third day, she mentioned how broke Brent was. And she also pointed out that boys just aren't as "naturally romantic" as girls. She was starting to sound desperate.

I almost felt sorry for her.

Almost.

Cary Retlin showed up at the table on the second day. "Having fun?" he asked, raising one eyebrow.

"Actually, I am," I answered.

He picked up a valentine-gram form. "So this is how it works. Do you guarantee confidentiality?"

"Well, we do our best. But we can't exactly *guarantee* anything." Cary was making me nervous. Why, I don't know. Maybe it was that eyebrow.

"How about if I take this home and type my message?" he asked.

"I — I don't think so," I stammered. I wasn't sure why, but that didn't seem right. Pete and I hadn't talked about it, but I didn't think he'd like the idea either. "These are supposed to be for fun," I said. "And they're valentines. They're supposed to be personal. Typing isn't personal."

"True," Cary agreed.

Just then, several other customers, including Jacqui Grant and Rose Marie Montey, arrived. I turned to help them, and when I turned back, Cary had left. I couldn't tell if he'd replaced the blank form on the pile or if he'd taken it with him. How annoying.

"Can I help you?" I asked Jacqui and Rose Marie.

Jacqui looked miffed. "Are you going to be at this table all day?" she asked. "Where's Pete?"

"Pete will be here," I said. "Our schedule is flexible."

"Hmph." Jacqui grabbed a couple of forms and started writing. For some reason, she didn't like my being around while she composed her valentine-grams. Was it because she was sending them to Robert? I could have told her there was absolutely nothing between us anymore, but she didn't ask. She just scribbled away, making sure to shield her writing from my eyes.

Rose Marie, on the other hand, seemed eager to let me see what she was writing. "Like this poem?" she asked, showing me a long rhyming mess about two hearts beating as one, sunsets on the beach, and kisses by the fireplace. "Romantic, isn't it?" she asked, giggling.

"Um, sure," I said. There was no denying that the poem included every romantic cliché I'd ever heard.

"I wrote it myself," Rose Marie told me proudly. "Well, actually some of it came from this card my aunt sent me last year, and I found some of it in an old book of poems I bought at the library's book sale. Have you ever been to their book sale? It's the best. And some of it's from a song my dad used to sing when I was a little girl —" Rose Marie paused for breath.

"Well, it's a great poem," I said, trying to cut her off gently. Rambling Rose was at it again. I've never met anyone who can talk as much, or as quickly, as Rose Marie.

Rose Marie and her boyfriend, Brian Hall, met through the school newspaper's personal ads, back when Claudia was in charge of that column. They've turned out to be a great pair — or at least that's what I'd always thought. I began to wonder how well things were going with them when I saw the stack of valentine-grams Rose Marie handed me after she'd spent practically her whole lunch hour at the table. She must have copied that poem over a dozen times. She handed me a pile of dollar bills and, with a cheery good-bye, left me to sort through her valentine-grams before adding them to the bag.

I noticed something strange right away. Not one was addressed to Brian.

Meanwhile, I should mention that Brian came by at the end of my shift and bought one valentine-gram, which he sent to Rose Marie.

"You learn a lot working here," I said to Pete when he showed up to take the bag to his locker. (He'd keep it there until the after-school shift, which he was covering.)

"No kidding," he said. "Like, can you believe that girls have been sending valentine-grams to Alan Gray?"

"Really?" I asked. I hadn't noticed that.

Pete nodded. "One of them is in Cokie's handwriting," he whispered, grinning. "Or at least I think it is."

Very interesting.

Another interesting thing? How nervous some boys seemed about the valentine-grams. Including Pete. Several times when we were working together I saw him acting all jumpy around one girl or another who had come to the table. Jim Poirier, a guy in our grade, seemed to be giving Pete a hard time about it. I overheard Pete telling him to cut it out. Boys can be so mean.

Robert was another boy who couldn't seem to deal with the valentine-grams. More than once I looked up to see him hovering around the area, but he never worked up the courage to actually approach the table. Was it the idea of Valentine's Day that he couldn't deal with? Or was it me? I'd learned a lot about human nature, and about my classmates, but Robert's behavior was a big mystery. And not just to me. As I was closing up shop for the day on Wednesday, Andi Gentile appeared and slipped me a note.

WE HAVE TO TALK ABOUT ROBERT.

CHAPTER 5

I couldn't imagine why Andi wanted to talk to me about Robert. After all, she knows better than anyone that he and I broke up. And she knows that I know about the two of them seeing each other before he and I had called it quits.

Andi and I were never best friends. For awhile, when I was first going out with Robert, I hung out with Andi and some of her friends. I thought they were sophisticated, more mature than my BSC friends. I feel ashamed of myself now, when I remember the way I turned my back on Mary Anne, Kristy, and the others in order to be part of that crowd. I hurt my friends badly, and though they were able to forgive me, I doubt they'll ever forget. I know I won't.

I also won't forget how badly my supposed new friends ended up treating me. They used me as a pawn in a shoplifting scheme, for one thing. And they brought liquor to a concert and got us all into trouble. Andi wasn't involved in those episodes, but Jacqui Grant was, along with a couple of other girls I no longer speak to.

Anyway, even though Andi and I were once friends, I can't say that we are now. I don't hate her, but I definitely don't trust her.

Still, I was curious. I'd been concerned about Robert, and I wondered what, if anything, Andi knew about what was going on with him.

"So, what's up?" I asked when I called her that night. I think it's clear to Andi how I feel, so I didn't waste time with a lot of phony "Hi, how are you?" stuff.

Andi hesitated. "Could we talk, um, in person?"

"Sure," I answered, a little disappointed. My curiosity wasn't going to be satisfied right away. "Just tell me where and when."

"How about before homeroom tomorrow? By the back entrance?"

"Fine," I agreed. "I'll be there." Pete was planning to cover the morning shift at our table, so I'd be free.

It's funny. I'm over Robert. But every time I think about him kissing Andi and Andi kissing him while he was still supposedly my boyfriend, I feel angry all over again. I mean, I knew at the time that Robert and I weren't going to last forever, or even for very much longer, but still. They could have had the decency to wait.

I didn't sleep well that night.

Which meant using a little extra concealer to cover up the circles under my eyes in the morning, some blush to make me look alert and happy, and a touch of lip gloss to keep me smiling. Ah, the wonders of makeup. Without it, I'd have to face Andi looking like the Creature from the Black Lagoon.

Andi was waiting for me when I arrived. "Hey," I said.

"Hi, Stacey," she answered. "Thanks for coming." She looked down at her feet. "I know we're not the best of friends," she began, after a long pause.

I didn't say anything. What was there to say? She was right.

"I mean, I know you have every reason to dislike me, or distrust me," she went on. I had a feeling she hadn't slept too well either. She must have been busy preparing this little speech. I gave her a closer look. Yup. She'd been using her under-eye concealer too.

"Look, Andi, forget it. Just tell me what's on your mind." I didn't intend to sound mean or impatient, but I think it may have come out that way. Andi looked crushed. "It's about Robert, right?" I asked. "What is it?"

"It's just that I'm worried about him," she began, finally. "I've tried sending him notes. I've tried talking to him. But I just can't seem to reach him." She paused. "Have you noticed how down he seems lately?"

I nodded.

"He barely says hello to me in the halls," she said. "And he even seems out of it when he's with his friends. You know?"

I nodded again. So Andi had seen the same behavior I had. "But what can I do?" I asked. "I mean, I've been concerned too, but —"

"I thought you could talk to him," she said. "You know him much better than I do. In fact, you probably know him better than anyone in school."

My mind flashed over some of the special times I'd shared with Robert: Our first date at the coffee shop. How he called me Toots. The way we danced together, and the way I felt when he held my hand. Or when we kissed.

"Stacey?" asked Andi.

"Oh — right," I said, coming out of my daydream. "I guess I do. Know him, I mean. I think I know him pretty well, in fact."

"So, could you talk to him?" asked Andi. "Try to find out what's wrong. I know he'll open up to you."

I wasn't so sure. But I was willing to try, and I told Andi so. She looked relieved. "Why do you care so much, anyway?" I asked. "Do you still like him?"

"No, it's nothing like that," she assured me. "It's just, well, you know Robert. He's a great guy, and even though it's over between us, I haven't stopped caring about him."

"I know what you mean," I said, giving Andi a smile. "I definitely know what you mean."

Just then, the bell rang for homeroom. "Thanks, Stacey," Andi called as we headed off in opposite directions.

"I'll let you know if anything comes of it," I said, "but don't expect too much."

During homeroom, I thought about Robert. The fact was, I felt the same way Andi did. Even though our romance was over, I still cared about him. So talking to him was the right thing to do, wasn't it? Sure it was.

But it wasn't so easy.

I spent the rest of that day keeping an eye out for Robert. I watched for him in the halls between classes. I cruised by his locker, oh, about five gazillion times. And at lunchtime, I lingered in the cafeteria line, hoping to run into him there. No such luck.

Naturally, the only time I saw him was when I didn't have time to talk. I was rushing out to relieve Pete at the valentine-gram table, so he could grab some lunch, when I spotted Robert sitting with his friends at a table in the corner of the cafeteria. As usual, the guys were laughing and carrying on — but once again, Robert seemed out of it.

While I was watching, Jacqui and her friend Sheila approached the table. There was no way I could hear what Jacqui was saying over the usual lunchroom noise-a-thon. But her body language made it perfectly clear: the way she held her head to one side, the way she smiled, the way she swayed from one foot to the other.

She was flirting.

Big-time.

I could read Robert's body language too: the folded arms, the lack of eye contact, the frown.

Here's what it said: "Bug off."

Even Jacqui couldn't miss the signals. She heard him loud and clear. She turned on her heel and practically stomped off, dragging Sheila behind her. I wondered if Robert could sense her frustration as well as I could.

I tried to catch Robert's eye. I gave him a little wave as I left the room, but I couldn't tell if he'd seen me. I didn't stop to find out either. I mean, I do care about Robert, but I wasn't going to chase him down.

After that, I didn't see Robert all day. I was busy with either the valentine-gram table or classes until the bell rang. After I'd visited my locker, I met up with Pete for our last valentine-gram session. There was a big crowd around the table by the time I arrived.

I peeked into the Gap bag and whistled. "This is turning out to be a great fund-raiser."

"And a great opportunity for all of us incurable romantics," I heard someone say. I turned to see Clarence King, the last person I would have used those words to describe, grinning at me. "King," as they call him (mainly because he'd cream anyone who called him Clarence), is your basic big, swaggering guy. He used to give Logan a hard time about being a member of the BSC. In King's world, boys don't baby-sit.

But I guess they do send valentine-grams, since Clarence was just finishing one up. He sealed it, addressed it, and stuffed it into the bag before I could see who it was for.

Plenty of other "romantics" showed up that afternoon, including Ben Hobart, who sent a valentine-gram to Mal. I was glad to see him, since I knew Mal had spent some time writing one to Ben.

Pete, thankfully, dealt with Cokie, who drifted by looking for Brent. Once again, I almost felt sorry for her when Pete informed her that no, he hadn't seen Brent all day.

Jacqui came by right after Cokie had left. Ignoring me, she flirted with Pete while she paid for and wrote out a quick valentine-gram. I had to wonder if she was really after Robert or if she just liked flirting in general.

Our next customer? Alan Gray. "How can we help you today, sir?" I asked, putting on my best salesperson act.

"I, um, actually," he began nervously, looking over my shoulder, "I was wondering . . ."

His voice was so low I had to lean forward to hear what he was saying. Jim Poirier had approached Pete and was teasing him about something again, but I tuned him out in order to listen to Alan. "What is it?" I asked. Alan seemed dead serious for once, and very jittery.

"Could . . . could I have one of my valentine-grams back?" he asked finally.

"You're kidding," I said.

He shook his head. "Never mind." He slipped away.

Rambling Rose returned and nervously wrote "one last message."

Meanwhile, Pete stood up. "Stacey, I have to go," he said. "There are only a few minutes left. Can you handle things here?"

Rose Marie had finally finished. I looked around and saw that the hall was almost empty. The buses must have left, and most kids had headed home. "Sure," I said. "I have a few valentine-grams to write anyway." I'd just realized that I'd forgotten to send valentine-grams to my BSC friends. Pete took off and I started writing.

I was just finishing the last one when something made me look up. There was Robert, standing right in front of me. I pushed the final valentine-gram into the bag. "Hi," I said.

"Hi," said Robert, looking serious. Finally, the moment had arrived. School was over, and the building was nearly empty. It was time to talk.

"Hey, am I too late?" asked Austin Bentley, appearing suddenly at the front of the table.

I sighed and held up one finger to Robert. "Just a sec," I mouthed. I turned to help Austin. He wrote out his valentine-gram and paid me. I put away his money and gathered up his valentine-gram plus a few others that had been scattered on the table. Then I looked up to tell Robert I was almost done.

But he was gone.

I sighed. Oh, well. If he didn't want to talk, he didn't want to talk. What could I do?

I started to put those last few valentine-grams into the bag.

But I couldn't.

Because the bag wasn't there.

CHAPTER 6

Thursday

Who thinks Valentine's Day is all about love and romance? Raise your hand. Notice how my hands are in my lap? That's because I know the truth. I learned it today, at the Hobarts'. Valentine's Day isn't about love. Or romance. It's about insecurity, disappointment, and a whole bunch of other nasty things. Kind of sad, really. But it doesn't have to be that way, does it? We have some planning to do.

Kristy was upset, there was no doubt about it. And who could blame her? Here she was, with this terrific idea for Valentine's Day, something that would make the holiday a fun and happy one for everyone. She'd done her homework, talking to the staff of the children's room at the Stoneybrook Public Library about the idea of creating a festival. Ms. Feld, the children's librarian, loved the idea. We had set up a meeting to discuss the details, and meanwhile we thought we'd start spreading the word to our charges.

Kristy, who was sitting for the Hobarts on Thursday afternoon, couldn't wait to see what they thought. She'd gathered the three younger Hobart boys (Ben was at a soccer game) and sat them down in the family room. For a second, Kristy wondered if Valentine's Day was celebrated in Australia. Maybe the boys didn't even know what it was all about. She might have to start out by explaining how the holiday began and what it had come to mean.

"I *hate* Valentine's Day," declared Johnny, interrupting Kristy's train of thought. At four, he's the youngest of the Hobart brothers. All four boys have reddish-blond hair and constellations of freckles scattered across their noses and cheeks. They also have the most endearing accents. At first we sometimes found it hard to understand what the Hobart boys were saying, but by now we've adjusted, as long as they don't use too many of their Australian slang terms such as "bonzer" (Australian for cool). Anyway, Kristy had no trouble deciphering his message, especially because it was accompanied by a huge scowl.

Kristy was just about to answer Johnny with the news that this Valentine's Day was going to be different, when James spoke up.

"So do I," he said, with a scowl that matched Johnny's.

Interesting, thought Kristy. She squashed the impulse to jump right in and tell the boys about the festival. Maybe it would make more sense to find out what the kids *didn't* like about Valentine's Day. That way, she'd have a better chance of planning an event that would make them happy.

"How about you, Mathew?" she asked. "How do you feel about Valentine's Day?"

Mathew blushed, a deep scarlet obscuring every one of his freckles. "I — I don't know," he said. "I think it's kind of scary."

Scary? Kristy didn't understand, but she didn't want to press Mathew. He already looked as if he might be about to burst into tears.

Instead, she turned back to Johnny. "Why do you hate Valentine's Day?" she asked him. It was hard to imagine how a four-year-old could have such strong negative feelings about a holiday.

"Because," said Johnny, sticking out his bottom lip, "I'm not in school yet. That means I won't get any valentines at all. Except maybe one from Mum." He made a face. "And James and Mathew and Ben will come home with bucketloads of cards. And they have cupcakes at lunchtime, and candy hearts, and everything." He scowled again and folded his arms over his chest.

Kristy felt a pang. She suddenly remembered what it had been like to be the younger sibling when her older brothers were in school and she wasn't. She'd been jealous of anything they brought home, even if it were something they were complaining about, such as homework. She knew it couldn't be easy for Johnny, being the youngest of four. She reached out and gave his shoulder a squeeze.

"And you, James?" she asked. "What don't you like about Valentine's Day?"

He blushed, though not as deeply as Mathew had. "Oh, it's silly," he said.

"You can tell me," Kristy replied. "I promise not to laugh or tell anyone else." She crossed her heart.

"Well," began James shyly. "There's this girl —"

"Woooo!" His brothers collapsed into giggles.

James looked helplessly at Kristy.

"Ignore them," she said. "Go on."

"It's just that I want to send her a card, but I can't find the right one. I've looked in all the stores, and nothing seems right. They're all too — too *something*. Some are all goopy, and some are too serious, and some are just too dumb."

"I know what you mean," Kristy said sympathetically.

"It's not like I'm in love with this girl or anything," James insisted. "I just think she's nice, and I'd like to be friends."

His brothers started "woo-ing" again.

Kristy tuned them out. She was thinking. It was a real eye-opener to hear what the boys thought about Valentine's Day. And if the Hobart boys felt this way, the chances were that other kids did too. She decided to find out. "Hey, guys," she said, "how about if we head over to see the Pikes? I'd like to find out what they think about Valentine's Day. And I happen to know they're home, because my friend is baby-sitting for them."

"Which friend?" asked Mathew in a tiny voice.

"Mary Anne," Kristy answered, and she saw that blush wipe out Mathew's freckles again.

"Will, um, all the girls be home?" asked James.

"I think so," said Kristy. "Want me to call first and find out?"

"NO! I mean, no, that's okay."

49

Aha, thought Kristy. So it's one of the Pike girls. But which one? She was dying to know, but she held her tongue.

Kristy called Mary Anne to make sure it was okay for her and the boys to come over, then left a brief note for Mrs. Hobart. (This is standard BSC procedure. We wouldn't want a parent coming home to an empty house and worrying.) Then she and the Hobart boys headed over to the Pikes'.

Vanessa answered the door. She's nine and on the dreamy side. She wants to be a poet when she grows up, and she often talks in rhyme. "Welcome friends, to our house so dear. We like it when you visit here!" she declaimed as she ushered everybody in.

Kristy gave James a quick glance. Was Vanessa the object of his affections? No, apparently not. His freckles were still showing; no blushing yet.

"Wait! Before anyone else asks you, let me," said Vanessa, blocking Kristy's way. "Don't you think three dollars is a fair price?"

"For what?" asked Kristy.

"For a poem. A really good poem that you could copy onto a valentine."

"Are you trying to sell poems to your brothers and sisters?" asked Kristy.

"Well, yes," admitted Vanessa. "But they keep complaining about my prices."

"If you want to be a poet you can't expect to be rich," Kristy told her. "Why don't you just give the poems away? Which is more important, fame or fortune?"

Vanessa had to stop and think about that one.

Meanwhile, Kristy and the boys headed into the kitchen, where the rest of the Pike kids were hanging out with Mal and Mary Anne.

"I don't care if there *are* other kinds of cards!" Claire — the youngest Pike, at five — was shouting as they came in. "I only wanted the Snoopy kind, and now they're gone, and everything's *rooned*!" She howled out that last word, on the verge of sobbing. Claire has a talent for tantrums.

"Maybe we can still find the Snoopy ones at some other store," Mal was saying. She glanced up at Kristy and rolled her eyes.

Nicky, who's eight, was sitting next to Claire. "Oh, be quiet," he said. "Having the right cards doesn't mean everything's okay anyway, you know." He picked up the top card from a stack in front of him. "I found the coolest racing-car cards, but now I don't even want to send them."

"Why not?" Kristy asked.

Nicky wouldn't answer.

"Because the triplets have been teasing him," Mary Anne explained. (The triplets are Mal's ten-year-old brothers: Adam, Byron, and Jordan.) "They told him it was uncool for a boy to send valentines to other boys, and that the girls would hate the cars. So now Nicky feels stuck."

"And I wasted two weeks' allowance too!" said Nicky.

"I'd like to get one of those cards," said Mathew shyly.

"So would I," Mary Anne said, giving Mathew a big smile. Kristy told me later that he turned so red she thought he'd explode.

"That boy has the biggest crush on you," she told Mary Anne, when the two of them had a brief moment alone later on.

"Oh, don't be silly," said Mary Anne. "But you know who *does* have a crush? Margo. She likes James. Actually, I shouldn't call it a crush. I think she just wants to be friends with him. But he won't even look at her, so she figures he can't stand her."

If Kristy had been paying attention, she might have realized that Margo had nothing to worry about. But her mind was on something else. "You know," she told Mary Anne, "I was going to tell the kids about our festival today. But I think I'll wait. After all I've seen this afternoon, I think we have some more planning to do. It's not going to be so easy to make Valentine's Day a happy holiday for everyone."

CHAPTER 7

"Pete, it's Stacey." I was still breathing hard. I had run all over the school, hoping to find the valentine-gram bag. No luck. After that, I had run all the way home and made a grab for the phone.

"What's up?" he asked. "You sound funny."

I tried to catch my breath. Then, forcing a casual tone, I asked the big question. "So, you have the bag, right?"

"Bag?" Pete asked. "Oh, you mean the bag with the valentine-grams?"

"Yes," I said with relief. "So you took it home?"

"What gave you that idea?" asked Pete. "I haven't seen it since I said good-bye to you at school this afternoon."

Gulp.

"In that case, I have some very bad news."

Pete was not happy to hear what I had to tell him. "Missing? How could it be missing? Did

53

you look under the table? What about the money, and the notebook?"

"I looked everywhere," I told him. "And the money and notebook are safe, for whatever that's worth."

"Oh, man," he moaned. "Do you realize what this means?"

"It means we're in big, big trouble," I answered. "And that everybody in school is going to want to kill us."

"And that we'll have to refund their money," Pete added, just to make things worse. "How could it have just disappeared?"

"I don't know," I said. "But it did."

"Maybe one of the other class officers picked it up," Pete suggested.

"That's it!" I said. "That *must* be it. I'll call everybody." I hung up without saying good-bye and dove for the phone book.

Ten minutes later, I was back on the phone with Pete. "That wasn't it," I reported. "None of them has seen the bag."

"This is a disaster," said Pete. "Come on, let's think. Who was hanging around the table today?"

"Alan!" I said. "Alan Gray. I bet he has something to do with this."

"Hold on," said Pete. "Everybody's always on Alan's case. I admit he's a goof, but I don't think he'd do something like this. Let's make a list of all the people who were there before we start blaming Alan."

Pete was right. "Okay," I said, thinking hard. "I'll write down the names. Who else?"

"Clarence King," said Pete.

"Right!" I said, remembering. "And Jacqui."

"And Cokie," he reminded me. "And Brian, and Rose, and —"

"Ben, but Ben couldn't have done anything wrong," I added, more to myself. "And Austin," I continued. "And Robert."

Our list was growing. If we wrote down the name of every person who'd been near the valentine-gram table, we'd have to list practically the entire student body of SMS. It wasn't going to be easy to narrow down the list of suspects. I said so to Pete.

"I know." He sighed. "We're dead."

"Let's make a deal," I suggested. "Let's try to keep this quiet for now. I mean, who knows? Maybe we'll find the bag at school tomorrow, and our worries will be over. Meanwhile, nobody but us has to know."

"You're right," agreed Pete. "I won't tell a soul."

It wasn't easy to keep the news to myself that night. I was dying to call my BSC friends and ask their advice. But a deal's a deal. I didn't go near the phone.

As if it mattered.

"How could you?" Cokie stood in my way, her hands on her hips.

"How could I what?" I asked. I was still a little groggy. Once again, I hadn't slept very well, and Cokie was pouncing on me even before homeroom.

"I thought you said the valentine-grams were supposed to be secret!"

Uh-oh. "Well," I began, not knowing where to start.

"Well, what do you have to say about *this*?" Cokie asked, shoving a piece of paper in front of my nose. I tried to focus.

NUMBER OF VALENTINES SENT FROM COKIE TO BRENT=12

NUMBER OF VALENTINES SENT FROM BRENT TO COKIE=0

SOME ADVICE FOR COKIE: GIVE IT UP! MAYBE BRENT DOESN'T LIKE BEING CALLED "SUGARBEAR"

"Sugarbear?" I asked, trying not to smile.

"It's not funny," said Cokie. Her face was pink and I suddenly realized that she was about to cry. She pointed down the hall. "See all those slips of paper on the floor and taped to the lockers? They all say the same thing.

This is *literally* all over the school." She stamped her foot. "*Do* something about it," she demanded.

I headed for Claudia's locker. At a time like this, a person needs her best friend.

"How *could* you?" asked Claudia when she saw me.

Oh, no. "Not you too," I said.

"If my valentines to Josh end up plastered all over the school, I'm going to die!" she exclaimed.

"They won't," I assured her quickly. "We'll figure out who stole the valentine-grams, and who spread the news about Cokie. Then —"

"Stole?" cried Claud. "STOLE? You mean to tell me you let someone *steal* them?"

"Well, I —" I began. But Claud had already jumped ahead.

"Anyway, there's nothing to figure out," she said. "Isn't it obvious? This is Cary Retlin's work."

She was right, of course. Why hadn't I seen it? I grabbed her by the sleeve. "Come with me," I said. "We're going to find Mr. Retlin and have a talk with him."

We only had a few minutes before homeroom. Fortunately, we had no trouble finding Cary.

Unfortunately, he had an excuse.

When I confronted him with the "evidence" — the slip of paper Cokie had given me — he put up both hands.

"Don't look at me," he said, shrugging. "I'd love to take credit for such a brilliant prank, but I didn't steal those valentine-grams. I wasn't even here after school yesterday. I left during last period because I had a dentist appointment. I can get a sworn affidavit from my hygienist if you want one. Or I can show you the new toothbrush she gave me."

Rats.

During homeroom, as I tried to hide my face behind my math notebook, Mr. Kingbridge, the assistant principal, made an announcement over the PA. "Will whoever stole the valentine-grams please return them to one of the eighth-grade class officers?" he said.

"I don't know if I'd take them back," Pete muttered. "I think it's just as well that they were taken."

Huh? What was Pete saying? Before I could ask him, the bell rang and he ran off to his first class.

Was I going to have to add Pete's name to my list of suspects?

That list grew and grew as I made my way through the day's classes. By lunchtime, my friends and I agreed that almost anyone in the school could be considered a suspect.

"It could be someone who sent a valentine-gram and then wished they hadn't," said Kristy, leaning back in her seat and making a face at her lunch.

"Or someone who didn't think he'd been sent one and was mad about it," added Mary Anne.

"Or someone who wanted to make Cokie look bad," put in Abby.

"That could be just about anyone," I said. It was true. Cokie's been nasty to so many people in school that nobody was feeling exactly sorry for her about what had happened.

I looked around at the crowd in the lunch-room, just to check out who was there and what they were up to. I didn't see Cary Retlin anywhere. Clarence King went swaggering by, and shot a straw wrapper at Alan Gray, who was sitting with Emily Bernstein. I saw Pete talk to Emily, then head back to his own table, which was near the one where Robert (looking as glum as usual) was sitting. At the next table sat Jacqui, who was sneaking peeks at Robert. Brian and Rose Marie must still have been having a tiff, because they were sitting at different tables.

I sighed. Any one of those people could be a suspect, as far as I knew.

Later that day, after the last bell, I was standing by my locker, trying to think about what to do next. The valentine-gram bag had not been turned in, and I was no closer to figuring out who could have taken it.

I felt a tap on my shoulder, and I whirled around to see Jacqui standing there.

She didn't look happy.

And she didn't say a word.

Instead, she just handed me a slip of paper.

GIVE IT UP, JACQUI! ROBERT DOESN'T LIKE YOU.

(AND NO, HE DOESN'T WANT TO "WALK ON THE BEACH AT SUNSET, HOLDING HANDS.")

I didn't know what to say. Obviously, the prankster had found one — or a few — of Jacqui's valentines to Robert. "I'm sorry, Jacqui —" I began. (I really was too.)

"I knew you were behind this!" she cried. "You just want to humiliate me, because you still like Robert!"

I was shocked. "No, I —" Then I looked around and saw that everyone in the hall was staring at us. And the looks they were shooting my way gave me a nasty feeling. Did people believe that I had something to do with the prank? The kids in the hall looked nervous, and suddenly I knew what they were thinking.

It was one thing when Cokie was the target of a prank. But who would be next?

"Jacqui, I didn't —" I began again, but she stormed off dramatically. I felt awful. Then I heard a voice behind me.

"Don't pay any attention to her."

I turned around. It was Robert.

CHAPTER 8

I felt my heart jump.

I can't explain why. Was it because Robert had startled me? Or was it something about hearing his voice at that moment?

For whatever reason, my heart jumped and I was speechless. I just stared at Robert, taking in his familiar features: his strong-looking shoulders; his thick, wavy light brown hair; his dark eyes.

Robert didn't seem to notice. He waved a hand. "Don't pay any attention to Jacqui," he repeated. "The fact is, I'm just not interested in her, and she was going to find out sooner or later, one way or another."

"But she's blaming me," I said. "And I had nothing to do with it."

"I know," said Robert. "Of course you didn't. You'd never hurt somebody on purpose."

That made me feel good. I only wished Robert could have said it over the PA, so everyone in school could have heard it.

"And it's not really your fault that somebody stole the valentine-grams," he continued. "There's no way you could have watched that bag every single second."

"If I'd had any idea that somebody wanted to steal them, I'd have kept that bag locked up," I said. My back was against my locker, and I slid down so I was sitting on the floor. "What a mess," I said, feeling tired. "Poor Cokie."

Robert sat down next to me and flashed me that killer smile of his. I'd almost forgotten about the dimples in his cheeks. "Poor Cokie?" he repeated. "I don't feel sorry for her at all. She's pulled nastier pranks on too many people in this school. Now it's her turn. She deserves even worse, if you ask me."

I thought about that. Maybe Robert was right. Still, being humiliated in front of the whole school had to hurt. I couldn't blame Cokie for being mad. For that matter, I couldn't blame Jacqui either. I just didn't want them to be mad at me. They should be focusing on the person who had stolen the valentine-grams, whoever that was.

"Hey, can I walk you home?"

Robert sounded hesitant, almost shy. He wasn't looking straight at me.

I realized the halls were empty. Everyone else had left school. Pretty soon Mr. Halprin and Mr. Milhaus, the custodians, would be starting to clean the halls and classrooms.

I looked over at Robert. "Sure," I said. Finally, we'd have some time to talk.

He stood and reached down a hand to help me up. I grabbed it and hauled myself to a standing position. Then I dusted off the back of my pants, checked to make sure my locker was locked, and smiled at Robert. "Let's go," I said.

Robert used to walk me home all the time when we were going out. I felt funny walking down the school's front steps with him. It was the same, only different. I wondered if he felt it too. I was just about to say something when Robert jumped up onto the metal railing and, holding his hands in the air, went sliding down to the bottom of the stairs. I smiled and shook my head. He probably *did* feel funny, but instead of talking about it, he had to act like a third-grader.

Boys.

He waited for me at the bottom of the stairs, and we started walking together. I knew I had to grab this chance to talk, but somehow I couldn't think of a way to start the conversation. I looked around, hoping for inspiration, and noticed a bird sitting in a tree. I pointed it out. "Look," I said. "Spring must be just around the corner if the robins are back already."

"That's not a robin," said Robert. "It's a sparrow. A few of them stay here all winter." He smiled at me fondly. "You're still a real New Yorker," he added.

I blushed. I guess it's true. I can't tell one bird from another, unless one of them is a pigeon. But if you asked me the difference between the A train and the D train (two of the lines in the New York City subway system), I could explain their routes, stop by stop. "I guess you can take the girl out of the city . . ." I began.

"But you can't take the city out of the girl," Robert finished. "That was always a little tough for me. I knew how much you love New York, but I never could learn to appreciate the place. It just seems noisy and crowded to me."

I thought of Ethan. He loves New York as much as I do. He says the city feeds his creative spirit. Our shared passion for Manhattan is part of our bond. "I wanted you to like the city," I told Robert. "But I understand why you don't."

Finally we were talking. "Robert," I began cautiously, "I want to ask you something."

He looked sideways at me. He'd picked up a handful of gravel and now he was tossing it, pebble by pebble, as he walked. "Shoot," he said.

I knew it would be a mistake to tell him

Andi had spoken to me. He'd be embarrassed if he knew we had been discussing him. So I just spoke for myself. "I've been . . . kind of worried about you lately."

"You have?" He tossed a pebble at a street sign, trying to act casual. "How come?"

"Well, you just don't seem yourself lately," I said. "You seem sort of — down. Sort of out of it."

Robert didn't say anything for about half a block. He threw pebbles as we walked silently along.

"Robert?" I asked finally.

"I don't know what to say," he replied. "First of all, you're right. I'm not feeling terrific. And second of all, thanks for noticing. And asking. I appreciate that." He flashed me a smile.

"So what's going on?"

"It's no big deal. I just haven't been feeling too excited about things lately. I mean, everything seems boring: school, my friends, TV. You know what I mean?"

"Sure," I said. "I guess I feel that way sometimes. But the feeling doesn't usually last too long."

"I bet I'll snap out of it soon," said Robert. He paused. "In a way, I'm glad Jacqui saw that note today. She's really been bugging me. I don't want to go out with her, but I couldn't figure out a nice way to say so."

"Now she knows," I said. "I have a feeling she'll leave you alone after this."

"Then there's my friends," Robert continued. Once he started talking, it was as if he couldn't stop. "They're okay, but sometimes I feel as if they're speaking some other language. They never talk about anything interesting. Just the same old stuff: girls, cars, disaster movies . . ."

"What about Alex?" I asked. I knew Alex Zacharias used to be one of Robert's best friends. "Don't you talk to him?"

Robert shrugged. "He's still pretty upset about his parents' divorce. And I don't know what to say to him. I want to help, but I can't. That makes me feel lousy."

I knew what he meant. That was exactly how I was feeling about him. I wanted to help, but I didn't know how. It was frustrating.

By then we'd walked all the way down Elm Street, and my house was in sight. I wasn't sure what else to say to Robert. There was an awkward pause in our conversation.

"So, I heard you're seeing somebody," Robert said suddenly. As soon as he'd blurted that out, he put his head down and stuck both hands in his pockets.

"Who told you that?" I asked. Somehow, I didn't want to talk about Ethan. But I didn't want to deny that I was seeing him either.

"Oh, it's just something I heard. You know how word goes around."

"That reminds me," I said, hoping to change the subject gracefully. "What have you heard about Brian and Rose Marie? From what I can see, they're not speaking to each other."

Robert seemed grateful to have another topic to talk about. "I don't know. Nobody knows what happened. But they sure aren't acting too lovey-dovey these days."

We chatted about Brian and Rose Marie and other SMS gossip for the rest of our walk. When we arrived at my house I thanked Robert for walking me home. In the old days, I would have invited him in for a soda. But I had the feeling he was eager to take off. And I had some thinking to do before I headed for that afternoon's BSC meeting. "See you, Robert," I said.

" 'Bye, Stace," he answered. "Thanks for the talk. I feel better already."

I wasn't sure whether to believe that or not, but I told him I was glad. Then he left, and I went inside to fix myself a snack.

As I rummaged through the fridge, I thought about Robert. Was it possible that he still felt something for me? He'd certainly acted uncomfortable when he'd asked me if I was seeing someone. I thought back to the last time

I'd seen him, when I was writing out my valentine-grams.

Had he thought I was writing them to a boyfriend? Exactly how curious was he about who that boyfriend was?

What about the way he'd said that Cokie deserved to be embarrassed? Just how strongly did he feel about that?

I remembered how relieved he had sounded about being rid of Jacqui. Had he been so bothered by her attention that he would do something drastic about it?

And last but not least, who was one of the last people I'd seen just before the valentine-gram bag was stolen?

Once I'd put all the facts together, it seemed as plain as day. I didn't want it to be true, but it was.

Robert was a suspect.

CHAPTER 9

"Order! Order!" Kristy was tapping her pencil on the desk.

Abby's voice rose above the racket in Claudia's room. "I'll have a BLT on rye with mayo. Hold the L, extra B. And make it snappy."

"Oh, ha-ha," Kristy said. "That joke is so old. Last time I heard it I fell off my dinosaur."

That cracked everyone up. We may be mature middle-school students, but that doesn't mean we can't appreciate a good third-grade joke.

Or, for that matter, third-grade food. Claudia had made fluffernutter sandwiches for everyone, and they were a big hit. (I, of course, was sticking with a handful of sourdough pretzels.)

Friday's BSC meeting was not a typical one. Oh, we took phone calls, and we spent a few minutes talking about our clients. Kristy filled us in on her job at the Hobarts', for example. But other than that we talked about nothing but the mystery of the stolen valentine-grams.

That's right, mystery.

I'd made it official by hauling out the mystery notebook and making an entry.

What's the mystery notebook? Well, the BSC members have a way of becoming involved in mysteries, probably because we all love them (Claud's not the only one who reads Nancy Drew books). In fact, we've solved quite a few. And when you're solving a mystery, one of the things you have to do is take lots of notes — on motives, suspects, stuff like that. Anyway, we figured it would make sense to keep those notes together in one place, instead of having them scattered around. The mystery notebook has made us into better, more efficient detectives.

But it was going to take more than efficiency to solve *this* case. For one thing, there were just too many suspects. Like, the entire student body of SMS. As we talked about the case that afternoon, one thing became obvious, and Kristy put it best.

"It could have been anyone," she said. "What we have to do is narrow it down to the most likely suspects and then start ruling them out, one by one. We'll end up with one or two major suspects and then the rest will be a snap."

"You make it sound so easy," said Mary Anne. "I'm not so sure we can solve this one."

"Of course we can," said Abby. "Look, let's

start by taking the main suspects, the way Kristy said. If you suspect someone, it's your job to start checking them out, first thing on Monday."

"Dibs on Brian and Rose Marie!" cried Claudia. "I'm dying to find out what's going on with them anyway."

"They're yours," said Kristy, making a note in the mystery notebook. "Meanwhile, I'll see if I can find out what Brent's been up to. He keeps a pretty low profile, and just because nobody's seen him near the valentine-gram table doesn't mean he's above suspicion."

"Speaking of suspicion," Abby put in, "how about if I check out Cary? I'm sure his dentist story checks out, but I still think we should keep an eye on him."

We all agreed with that.

"I hate to say this, but I'm wondering about Pete," Mary Anne said softly. "I mean, there he is, in the middle of everything. If you think about it, he's in the perfect position to fake a robbery."

Hmm . . . I hadn't thought of that. Earlier that day I'd mentioned to Pete that my friends were on the case, investigating the theft of the valentine-grams. He seemed glad, and said he'd keep his eyes open for suspects. Did that mean he wasn't one himself? Not necessarily. He could have been trying to throw me off by acting casual. "Good plan, Mary Anne," I said.

Mal and Jessi said they'd just float around school, checking out anything suspicious. "Nobody notices us sixth-graders," said Jessi. "We can spy on everyone."

I was planning to keep an eye on all the major suspects myself, since I'd be working at the valentine-gram table again. Yes, we were open for business once more. We'd made an announcement over the PA that morning, saying that anyone who'd already sent a valentine-gram could come by the table to fill out a replacement (we had their names in our notebook). Nobody was thrilled by our solution, since it wasn't easy for them to recreate their masterpieces, but we didn't know what else to do. When I listened to kids in my homeroom grumbling about it, I became even more determined to find those missing messages in time for Valentine's Day. Which meant it was time for the BSC members to move into high gear on our investigation.

Verrrry interesting. . . who would have thought things would work out this way? Maybe a certain person with the initials C. M. ?

Kristy had the surprise of her life on Monday morning. She'd planned to hang out in the hall near Brent's locker before homeroom, hoping to catch a glimpse of him and start on her surveillance. She caught a glimpse of him, all right.

A glimpse of him and Cokie together. And they weren't fighting this time. Instead, they were coming very, very close to breaking the SMS rule against public displays of affection.

They were sitting on the windowsill.

He was gazing into her eyes.

She was gazing back.

And the two of them appeared to be exchanging whispered sweet nothings.

Kristy crept closer, trying to hear over the usual roar of a crowded hallway.

"I just felt so awful for you," Brent was saying as he stroked her hand. "Having your private feelings splashed all over the school."

"It was humiliating," Cokie answered. "But you know what, Sugarbear? Now that we've made up, I don't care anymore."

Awww . . . For a second, even Kristy was moved. But then she stopped to think. Cokie had been upset about the fight she and Brent had had. She'd written all those valentine-grams. Clearly, she'd wanted to make up with him.

Could she have been so desperate to have him back that she'd embarrass herself in front of the whole school?

Franckly, I'm dissapointed. After all, I brot Brain and Rose Mary together. I used to feel kind of like there ferry godmother. But now I gess its all over.

Claudia didn't have too much luck observing Brian and Rose Marie. At least, she didn't have much luck observing them *together*. She saw Brian walking in the halls, sitting in the cafeteria, and heading into classrooms. And she saw Rose Marie in all the same places.

But never at the same time.

The two of them seemed to be doing a great job of avoiding each other. "It was almost like when you have two magnets that don't stick together," Claudia explained with her usual grasp of scientific principles. "Even if you tried to make them meet, you couldn't."

Asking around, Claudia discovered that it was pretty much common knowledge that Brian and Rose Marie had broken up for good. At least, that was what Rose Marie's friends said. Brian's friends left out the "for good" part. According to them, Brian wanted to get back together with Rose Marie. "She's the best thing that ever happened to him," explained Rick Chow. "He doesn't want to let some stupid fight end it all."

Claudia never did find out what the fight had been about. Only Brian and Rose Marie knew that, and neither of them was talking.

Claudia's investigation didn't turn up any new information about the missing valentine-grams. But, according to her, neither Rose Marie nor Brian was a suspect. "They're too busy avoiding each other," she explained.

Poor Pete. It must be torture to be so shy. I can certainly relate — although I would never let my feelings drive me to a life of crime.

Mary Anne had never imagined herself hanging around outside the boys' bathroom, but we BSC members will do almost anything in order to solve a mystery. And, in the process of tailing Pete Black, Mary Anne ended up discovering that a bathroom can be a pretty great spot for detective work. Why? Well, because it's a place where kids feel comfortable speaking freely, knowing members of the opposite sex can't hear them. Supposedly.

Mary Anne had been following Pete and his friend Austin through the halls. She was just about to give up her surveillance, since they weren't talking about anything besides some boring basketball game, when the two of them stopped in at the boys' bathroom. The outer door was open, so Mary Anne stationed herself next to it and waited. What she heard surprised her.

"So, did you send it?" asked Austin.

"Uh-huh," answered Pete. "But then I almost wished I hadn't. And I'm almost glad it won't be delivered now, since they were stolen. She probably would have thought it was dumb."

"No, she wouldn't," said Austin. "Emily would love it, trust me."

"I told you not to say her name!" cried Pete. Then, more quietly, he added, "I told you I don't want anybody to know I have a crush on Emily Bernstein."

Outside, Mary Anne put her hand over her mouth. This was big news! When Pete and Austin came out of the boys' room, Pete's face was flaming. Mary Anne quickly turned the other way and walked off, thinking hard.

So Pete liked Emily. That was sweet. But it sounded as if he regretted sending that valentine-gram to her. There was only one question on Mary Anne's mind: Did he regret it so much that he had stolen the valentine-gram bag just to get it back?

I know what you mean about bathrooms, Mary Anne. We agree 100%. We did some Lavatory

Listening ourselves and found out something very intriguing . . . .

Mal and Jessi didn't know what to make of the comment they overheard in the girls' bathroom between fifth and sixth period. But they knew it belonged in the mystery notebook, because it had to do with the valentine-grams.

Grace Blume was talking. And, of all people, Alan Gray was the topic of conversation. Grace was telling someone (Jessi and Mal, hiding in a stall, didn't see who it was) that she was sorry the valentine-grams weren't going to be delivered. "I'd have given anything to see the look on Alan Gray's face when he read his!" she said. Then she must have washed her hands and left, because Jessi and Mal heard nothing more than the sound of running water and the slamming of a door.

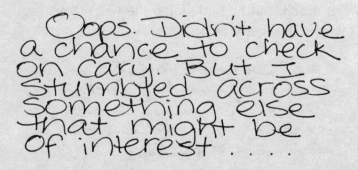

Oops. Didn't have a chance to check on Cary. But I stumbled across something else that might be of interest . . . .

Abby had such a busy day that she never found a chance to follow Cary around and spy on him. Finally, at the end of the day, she was dashing through the halls looking for him when she discovered that the valentine thief had struck again.

One entire hall of lockers was plastered with copies of passionate valentine-grams from Clarence King to Rose Marie, and vice versa.

Abby couldn't believe her eyes. *This* was big news. And maybe it explained Brian and Rose Marie's breakup.

Then, for the first time all day, Rose Marie and Brian appeared together, at the end of the hall near Brian's locker. Abby told us later that Rose Marie was begging Brian to believe that she'd never sent a valentine-gram to Clarence King. "She told him she'd sent a few others, just as pranks, but that she'd *never* send one to King, even as a joke," Abby told us later. "Brian didn't look convinced. And I'm not either. I'm not sure what it has to do with the missing valentine-grams, but I'll tell you one thing. Did you ever hear the expression 'the plot thickens'? Well, this is one plot that's getting thicker all the time."

MONDAY
OKAY, KRISTY, I HAVE TO ADMIT YOU
WERE RIGHT. SO I'LL DO IT HERE AND NOW,
IN WRITING. KRISTY WAS RIGHT.
AT FIRST I THOUGHT THE IDEA WAS
RIDICULOUS, BUT THE FACT IS, IT WORKED.
WE FOUND OUT WHAT WE NEED TO KNOW.
AND THE VALENTINE'S DAY FESTIVAL
IS GOING TO BE A BIG WINNER, GUARANTEED.

Logan's entry in the BSC notebook must have made Kristy's day. Everyone likes being told they were right. Kristy *loves* it. She thrives on it. She lives for it. And if nobody else will do it, she does it herself. But this time she didn't have to, because Logan was nice enough to write it down for everyone to see. I wouldn't be surprised if Kristy blows up a copy of that page to post on her bedroom wall.

Anyway, you must be wondering what she was right about. I'll explain.

After the experience she had with the Pike and Hobart kids, Kristy realized that planning a Valentine's Day festival wasn't going to be easy. She wanted to make sure to create a day that all the kids would enjoy. She'd learned a lot about what kids *didn't* like about the holiday, but what was the best way to find out what they *did* like?

Amazingly, the answer came to her during dinner only two days later. Kristy's mom was talking about work, and she mentioned something about a "focus group." At first Kristy wasn't paying much attention. Her mind was focused on her dinner, which was lasagna, one of her favorites. But as her mom kept talking, what she was saying began to sink in. Kristy asked some questions about focus groups and realized that the concept was exactly what she'd been looking for.

What's a focus group? Kristy's mom explained it to Kristy, and Kristy explained it to us. It's very simple. A focus group is a tool businesses use to find out how the public feels about their products. They bring in a bunch of "regular citizens" and sit them down in a room together. Then they ask them questions. "How do you feel about New, Improved Maxi-Clean for Small Dogs?" "Would you recommend Spring-Fresh Mitten Deodorizers to a friend?" "What words would you use to describe the flavor of Chocolate-Covered Fish Zingies?"

Sometimes researchers just watch the people talk among themselves, from behind a one-way mirror.

Anyway, if it turns out that the average young male snowboarder thinks Chocolate-Covered Fish Zingies taste "awesome, dude," then the business will know they should advertise their product in snowboard magazines. Or if most dog owners are more interested in a cleaning product for their *large* dogs, the Maxi-Clean people will know they have to work on creating one.

Okay, now fast-forward to Monday afternoon, and the first-ever BSC focus group. Purpose: to plan the best Valentine's Day festival ever. Location: Mary Anne's barn. On hand: four sitters and their charges.

Kristy couldn't be there (she had a preseason girls' softball team meeting), so she asked Logan to be in charge. He had a sitting job with the Hobarts, and Mary Anne was sitting for Matt and Haley Braddock (he's seven, she's nine). They invited Jessi, who was sitting for her sister, Becca (she's eight), and Charlotte Johanssen (also eight, and one of my favorite clients) and Mal, who promised to bring along as many of her siblings as she could round up.

"I still think this is the dumbest thing I ever heard of," Logan whispered to Mary Anne as they set up a big circle of folding chairs.

"Give it a chance," Mary Anne whispered back. "Who knows? Maybe it'll work."

Just then, Matt ran to Mary Anne and made some motions with his hands. Haley, who had followed him, explained. "He wants to know what we're doing today," she said. Matt is profoundly deaf and uses American Sign Language to communicate. Every BSC member has learned to sign a little, but for complicated things we need help. Haley is one of his best interpreters.

"We're going to talk about Valentine's Day," she said. Haley translated.

Matt nodded. He didn't look too thrilled.

Mary Anne had to admit that it didn't sound

83

like much fun. "Then we'll have some cookies," she added. She and Logan had made chocolate chip cookies the day before. Kristy's mom had explained that focus group participants were usually paid or given gifts for their trouble.

Matt's face brightened. His hands flew.

"He wants to know if he can have five," Haley said, laughing. "He's a cookie monster."

Mary Anne promised that there were plenty of cookies to go around.

By then, everyone had arrived. The noise level in the barn was rising fast. Logan put two fingers into his mouth and whistled loudly. "Hi, everybody!" he said when he had their attention. "How about if we all sit down in a circle?"

Mary Anne, Jessi, and Mal helped to herd the kids toward the chairs. Then there was a flurry of seat switching. Vanessa *had* to sit next to Becca and Charlotte. Nicky didn't want to be anywhere near Jordan, Adam, and Byron, because they were in a teasing mood. Matt needed to sit near Haley, so she could sign for him, and she wanted to sit near Becca, Charlotte, and Vanessa, which meant that James and Johnny had to pick up and move. Mathew hovered near the circle, waiting to see where Mary Anne was going to sit. (By then it had become pretty obvious that he had a crush on her.) Claire saved a seat for Margo, but as soon as

Margo sat down, James (who was in the seat next to her) popped up and, blushing, dashed to the other side of the circle.

"Ready to have a seat?" Logan asked Mathew, smiling.

"Leave me alone!" said Mathew, turning his back on Logan.

Logan raised his eyebrows. "What's going on?" he mouthed to Mary Anne.

"Tell you later," she mouthed back. Then she took a seat and patted the chair next to her. "Mathew, want to sit here?" she asked.

His face turned red, then white. "Um, okay," he said, gulping. He sat down gingerly, shooting shy glances on Mary Anne's other side.

Jessi and Mal found seats too, and for a second everybody was quiet as they looked around the circle at each other. Then Adam broke the silence — with a loud belch.

"Good one!" said Jordan, giving him a high five.

"Oh, ew," said Charlotte.

"Boys are so gross," said Becca.

"At least we don't have cooties, like girls do," yelled Nicky.

Adam, Jordan, and Byron started a belching contest.

"Make them stop," pleaded Margo, who is notorious for her weak stomach. "I'm afraid I'm going to hurl."

Logan gave another of his loud, shrill whistles. Then he put his hands in a T shape. "Timeout," he said. "We're here for a reason, you know," he continued, as soon as the belching and yelling had stopped. "How about if we get started?"

"What are we supposed to do again?" asked Nicky. "Mal told me, but I don't remember."

"We're just going to talk about Valentine's Day," Logan explained. "We already know there's a lot you don't like about it, but we want to know what you *do* like."

Silence.

Then Margo spoke up in a shy voice. "I like it when Vanessa writes me my own special poem," she said.

Vanessa smiled, looking extremely pleased. "Thanks, Margo," she said. "And I like it when you give me a card you made yourself."

"Making cards is fun," said Claire. "And you don't have to worry about the kind you want being sold out at the store either."

"I like it when I get tons and tons of cards," said Haley. Next to her, Matt signed a quick sentence. "So does Matt," she said. "But he doesn't like pukey romantic ones," she added quickly, as Matt signed some more.

"I don't think Valentine's Day has to be about romantic stuff," said Becca. "I think it's about friendship. I like to send cards to all my friends, but that doesn't mean I want to *marry* them."

Everybody loudly agreed with that.

"And I think it's good if you don't leave anybody out," said Margo. "So nobody's feelings are hurt. If you give cards at all, you should give them to everybody in your class. That was the rule my teacher made last year."

"And I don't think Valentine's Day has to be about just cards," put in James. "In Australia, we always had cupcakes and candy hearts and all."

"I think Valentine's Day could also be a time to show somebody that you appreciate them," said Vanessa. "Like, I gave my mom a card last year."

"And you can make things besides cards and cupcakes," put in Becca. "My cousin does crafts for Valentine's Day. Once she sent me a beautiful ceramic heart. I'd like to learn how to make one."

Logan, busy scribbling notes, took a break to glance at the other sitters and give them the thumbs-up sign. The focus group was working. If we paid attention to the information the kids were giving us, we could create the best Valentine's Day festival ever.

CHAPTER 11

"The kids were amazing!" On Thursday morning, as we walked to school together, Mal was still full of news about the focus group. She and Mary Anne were excited about the festival.

The sitters who had run the focus group had told us about it at Monday's meeting. We'd learned so much from the kids, and it had really helped with our planning for the Valentine's Day festival, which would take place that afternoon. I hadn't been in on much of the planning, since my friends had sort of excused me from helping out (I was way too busy with the valentine-gram business). But I'd been there for Wednesday's meeting, when we discussed the final details, and I knew it was going to be a great event.

"We still have a lot of work to do," said Mary Anne, "but this is one party that's guaranteed to please our charges."

"That's terrific," I said. And I meant it. But I couldn't seem to match their level of enthusiasm. Don't get me wrong. I love a party as much as the next person, especially if it involves a room full of happy kids. It's just that my mind was on other matters.

My friends had worked hard all week long, tailing suspects and collecting clues. But today was going to be different. We were no closer to solving the "mystery of the stolen hearts," as Mal had taken to calling it, and I could see that my BSC friends now had something else on their minds.

I couldn't depend on them for help anymore. If I was going to find the missing valentine-grams — and solve the mystery of who had taken them, and why — I was going to have to do a lot of the work myself. And I didn't have much time.

Stacey McGill, solo detective.

I didn't mind, really. I knew I could count on my friends to help, if and when I really needed them. Meanwhile, my job was clear. I had to examine every suspect, investigate every lead, check out every clue.

My first mission? To follow up on my suspicions about Robert. I didn't like having him on my suspect list, and I wanted to clear his name. But how?

I decided to deal with the problem head-on.

Now that Robert and I had finally had our talk, maybe he'd be more approachable. And if so, why not just flat-out *ask* him if he'd been involved? One thing I happen to know about Robert is that he's not a good liar. And he has never been able to lie to me. If he was telling the truth, I'd know it.

As Mal and Mary Anne and I approached the entrance to SMS, I spotted Robert and his friends hanging out near the flagpole. I told my friends I'd see them later and headed toward Robert. He saw me coming and walked toward me.

"Hi," he said. He looked happier today. Maybe all he'd needed was to talk about his feelings a little.

"Hi, yourself," I said. We smiled at each other. "Hey, Robert," I said casually, "I wanted to ask you something."

"Haven't I heard those words before?" he replied, teasing me a little. I remembered then that I'd used the exact words to begin our talk the other day.

"I guess you have," I said, laughing. "But this is a *different* something."

"Go ahead," he said. He didn't look nearly as nervous as he had before.

"I don't know how to ask you this," I began, "so I'll just put it as simply as I can. Did you have anything to do with the stolen valentine-grams?"

"What?" Robert asked. "What are you talking about?" He looked completely shocked.

"You know, the *val*entine-grams," I repeated.

"I know, I know. I mean, how could you even think I would do a thing like that?"

"I — I just thought maybe you couldn't figure out any other way to let Jacqui know you weren't interested," I said lamely. The idea seemed ridiculous as soon as I'd said it out loud.

"You're crazy, Stacey McGill," said Robert, laughing. He shook his head. "I know you love to solve mysteries, but this time you're going to have to keep working. I didn't do it, and I don't know who did. But if I find out anything, I'll be sure to let you know." He walked off, still shaking his head.

Oh, well. I knew he wasn't lying. The good news was that Robert was off the suspect list. The bad news? The suspect list was still about a mile long.

I headed into school to meet Pete at the valentine-gram table. We'd taken care of most of the replacement valentine-grams by now, but we still had plenty of customers, especially since we'd put up a big sign promising that there was no way we'd let the thief strike again. Pete had bought a pair of plastic handcuffs at the toy store, and he'd made a big show of locking the *new* valentine-gram bag to his wrist during the hours we were open. Between times, we stored the bag in the principal's office, where it would be safe.

As we worked together that morning, I kept stealing glances at Pete. So far, he was still a suspect. Had he really been so nervous about sending a valentine-gram to Emily that he'd staged the burglary?

When the bell rang for homeroom, I watched as Pete shoved a stack of valentine-grams into the bag. Suddenly, it came to me. Why would Pete steal the valentine-gram bag? He had total access to it. If he'd really wanted his valentine-gram back, he could have rummaged through the bag to find it — anytime at all.

Scratch another suspect.

The list was growing shorter, little by little.

In English class, I spotted the next person on my list. Cary Retlin. Supposedly he had an alibi. But isn't that "I was at the dentist" line the oldest one in the book? I decided to check it out. First, I had to find out which dentist he went to. After class, I approached Cary. "Hey," I said, trying to sound friendly and concerned, "how did it go at the doctor's the other day? Everything okay?"

(Notice how I said "doctor." I learned that from *Columbo*. Ever watch *Columbo* reruns? They're great. The detective on that show always acts clueless, which sets the suspect's mind at ease. Then he goes in for the kill.)

"I wasn't at the doctor," Cary said without

batting an eye. "I was at the dentist. And if you don't believe me, you can check it out. I go to Dr. Rice. His number's in the phone book. Just look under 'alibi.' "

Oh. I'd been prepared to have to trick him into telling me his dentist's name. Cary was letting me know that *he* knew what I was up to.

"I believe you, I believe you," I said, putting up my hands and backing away.

Ha. As soon as I was out of his sight, I sprinted for the phone. But Dr. Rice's receptionist confirmed what Cary had told me. Another suspect cleared.

As I hung up, a notice pinned to the bulletin board next to the phone caught my eye. I looked closer. "Oh, no," I groaned, pulling it down, I read it carefully.

VALENTINE-GRAM

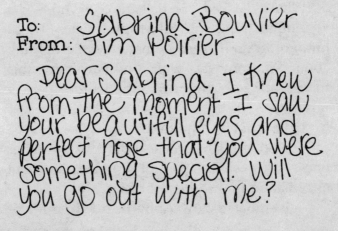

To: Sabrina Bouvier
From: Jim Poirier

Dear Sabrina, I knew from the moment I saw your beautiful eyes and perfect nose that you were something special. Will you go out with me?

Oh, lord. Perfect nose? If this valentine-gram were plastered all over the school, Jim was never going to live it down. Somebody had used a photocopy machine to copy the actual valentine-gram this time, so there was no doubting that it was the real thing.

I walked down the hall on my way to lunchtime duty at the valentine-gram table, pulling down every copy I saw. There were plenty of them. Poor Jim. "Check this out," I said to Pete as I slid into my seat.

Pete glanced at it. "I've seen it already," he said shortly.

That's when I remembered the disagreements I'd overheard between Jim and Pete. I asked him what they'd been about.

"Nothing, really. Jim was going to stuff the valentine-gram bag with prank valentines," said Pete.

"What?" I asked. "So he's the one who —"

"I don't think so," interrupted Pete. "I told him not to do it. That's what we were fighting about. And anyway, would he have done this to himself?" He pointed to the words "perfect nose."

"I guess not," I admitted.

"That doesn't mean he didn't do the other ones," Pete said. "For all I know, he went ahead and pranked his heart out."

I remembered how Abby heard Rose Marie

telling Brian that the valentine-grams between her and Clarence King were made up. Maybe she was telling the truth after all.

I took another look at the copied valentine-gram — and that's when I saw it. Something that made my heart race. "Whoa," I said to myself. I wasn't ready to share my discovery with Pete. This was a job for the BSC. "I — I have to go," I blurted out to Pete. Then I ran into the cafeteria, looking for my friends.

Kristy, Claudia, and Mary Anne were sitting at our usual table, and I saw Abby working her way across the crowded room, tray in hand. Great. Except for Jessi and Mal, the whole team was on hand.

"Stripes!" I said, throwing the copied valentine-gram down onto the table. "We have to find the stripes."

"What are you talking about?" asked Kristy, looking at me as if I'd gone nuts.

"Perfect nose?" asked Abby, who'd arrived and plunked down her tray. "Sabrina Bouvier has a perfect nose? You could have fooled me."

"Forget the nose," I said. "Look at the stripes."

"I see!" said Mary Anne. "Look," she said to the others. She pointed at the copy. The actual valentine-gram was smaller than the paper it had been copied on. "Look at this faint imprint of a hand and part of a sleeve. Whoever copied this was wearing a striped shirt. And if the copy was made today, that person would *still* be wearing the shirt."

"Bingo!" I shouted. "So let's find him!"

"Or her," Kristy pointed out.

"Right," I said. "Or her, or them. Or it. I don't care. Let's just find the person who did this — now!"

CHAPTER 12

"Right," said Kristy. "Let's fan out. Every-body look for stripes!" She pushed back her chair and stood up, ready for action.

"Wait a second," I said. I was in a hurry too, but by then I'd collected my thoughts enough to know we had to have a plan. "First of all, let's decide who's going where. And we have to think about what we'll do if we see someone wearing stripes."

Mary Anne spoke up. "I don't think we should confront the person right away. Wouldn't it be better if we could catch the culprit in the act?"

"Yeah," said Claudia. "Like, when he or she's making copies or posting them in the halls."

"Definitely," agreed Abby. "Let's just say that if we spot stripes, we'll report back to Stacey."

"Great," I said. "I'll be cruising the halls and I shouldn't be hard to find. Now, who wants to check the library?"

"I will," called Mary Anne. "I go there a lot after lunch anyway, so it won't look suspicious."

"I'll check the gym," volunteered Logan, who had stopped at our table to visit Mary Anne and stayed when he heard what was going on.

"Actually," I told him, "there's another place I need you to check. Abby, could you go to the gym instead?"

Abby nodded. "Sure," she said. "My free-throw shot could use a little work anyway."

"Where do you want me to go?" asked Logan.

"Somewhere the rest of us wouldn't be able to go," I said with a little grin. "The boys' bathrooms."

"Right," said Logan, laughing. "I'll cover that area. No problem."

"I can check the art room," said Claudia.

"Excellent," I said. "What about you, Kristy?" I asked.

She was still standing. "I'll look around outside, on the school grounds. There are always some kids out there at lunchtime, even if it's cold."

"That covers it," I said.

"Um," Mary Anne said gently. "Isn't there one place we're forgetting?"

I frowned. As far as I knew, we'd mentioned

all the popular lunchtime hangouts. "I don't think so," I said. Then I saw Mary Anne's gaze travel around the cafeteria, which was still about half full. "Oh!" I said, suddenly understanding. "Duh." I smacked myself on the forehead and made a goofy face. "The cafeteria. Of course."

My friends and I spread out to do a quick check of the lunchroom. It was strange to be looking only at people's clothes and not their faces. I couldn't have told you who I passed as I walked around, but I could have given a complete report on what they were wearing.

We met again near the main doors.

"Floral prints certainly are big this season," commented Claudia.

"So are solids," added Abby.

"But not a stripe in sight," said Mary Anne, sighing. "This may be harder than we think."

"Actually," I said, "the fact that nobody's wearing stripes makes it *easier*. This way, the stripe wearer will really stand out."

"Good point," said Kristy, who was shifting impatiently from foot to foot. "Now, what are we waiting for?"

My friends were back on the case. I told you I could count on them. "Nothing," I said with a big smile. "Let's go!" I pushed open the doors.

We fanned out, looking like the BSC version of a SWAT team. The others took off quickly, heading for their destinations. But I strolled along at a relaxed pace, since I wasn't going anywhere in particular. My plan was to walk the halls, check every person I saw for stripes.

Now, I'm a friendly person, and normally I like to make eye contact with people and say "hi" to the ones I know. But that day, people must have thought I was in a terrible mood. I didn't smile at a single person. My mind was on stripes, and nothing else mattered.

I saw plaids.

I saw lots of black.

I saw tie-dye.

I even saw one shirt that was printed all over with Yorkshire terriers. (Don't ask.)

But I didn't see a single stripe.

Until, suddenly, my field of vision was filled with them. Blue and black ones, to be exact. My heart skipped a beat.

"Stacey?"

I looked up slowly, dying to see who was wearing the striped shirt. Finally, the culprit was about to be unveiled.

"Is something wrong?" It was Mrs. Downey, the principal's secretary.

My heart resumed its normal rhythm. "I'm fine," I answered, hoping my disappointment wasn't evident in my voice. Then I took a second look at her. This woman had easy access to a copy machine. Could she have — ? "No way."

"What?" asked Mrs. Downey.

Oops. "I mean, no, nothing's wrong," I said, trying to cover for myself. I hadn't meant to speak out loud. I backed away from her and continued down the hall, ignoring her bewildered look.

Mrs. Downey was a hard-working, mature adult. She was not the valentine-gram thief. It had to be a student. Who else would pull the kind of pranks we'd been seeing?

I went over the list of possible suspects in my head. There were Cokie and Brent and Rose Marie. I'd cleared Cary, Pete, and Robert. Clarence King was still under suspicion, though, and so was Jacqui. I couldn't forget Austin.

And how could I possibly check each SMS student for stripes, before they all went home and changed? For that matter, what if someone had made that copy the day before, and wasn't even wearing stripes today? Or what if the stripes had been on a jacket? My head was spinning.

Suddenly, I felt a little tired. The fact was, time was running out. I'd hardly narrowed down the suspect list at all. And the list didn't even include dozens of other kids who could easily have stolen the valentine-grams.

"What's the matter, Stacey?"

I looked up to see Rose Marie. She was not wearing stripes. (In fact, she was wearing a very nice olive-green sweater with a denim miniskirt. Mentally I gave her an A+ for fashion.)

"You look bummed," she said.

"I am," I confessed. "I just can't figure out who stole the valentine-grams. Who would pull all these pranks?"

I figured Rose Marie would still be feeling angry at whoever posted those valentine-grams she wrote to Clarence King. But instead, she seemed angry at me.

"It was just a joke," she said. "Why are you making such a big deal about it?"

"Huh? You took it as a joke when your valentine-grams to King were plastered all over the walls?"

"Oh," she said. Now she looked confused. "I thought you were talking about something else."

"Like what?" I asked.

"Nothing, really," she said. "Nice blouse," she added quickly.

"Thanks," I said. "But go on. What did you think I was talking about?"

She looked embarrassed. "I thought you found the prank valentine-grams I sent."

"You sent some too?" I asked. What was going on here? Had the whole school gone crazy?

"But who —" I began. I was about to ask her who she'd sent prank valentine-grams to when Claudia came running toward me. She pulled me aside.

"Cary!" she whispered, trying to catch her breath.

"What about him?" I asked. After I'd checked out Cary's alibi, I'd forgotten about him.

"He's wearing stripes!" Claudia cried. "I just remembered. I saw him right after homeroom."

Suddenly, an image of Cary came into my mind. I'd spoken to him only a couple of hours earlier. As soon as I thought about it, I remembered too. He'd been wearing a green-and-yellow-striped turtleneck. "But I cleared him," I said. "He really was at the dentist that day."

Claudia shook her head. "Doesn't matter," she said, still gasping for air. "I thought about it while I was looking for you. Don't you remember, when we first confronted him? Before we'd even told him any details about the theft, he said he was at the dentist after school."

"And this proves — ?" I asked.

"How did he know what time the valentine-grams were stolen?" Claudia crossed her arms, looking triumphant.

I gulped. Claudia was right. Cary had given me a good alibi: *too* good.

"Hey, Stacey, I have to go," called Rose Marie. "See you later!" She walked off, waving.

"Okay, see you," I called back distractedly. I could hardly even remember what we'd been talking about. I only had one thought on my mind. "Let's go," I told Claudia. "We have to catch a thief."

CHAPTER 13

Claudia glanced around wildly. "Where do we start?" she asked. She was still flushed from running to find me. "He could be anywhere."

"We need to split up," I said. I checked my watch. We had thirteen minutes before our lunch period was over.

"You take the cafeteria," I told Claud. "He could have arrived after we left. And check every hallway and corner between here and there. I'll take everything in the other direction."

"Check," said Claudia. "Should we syncopate our watches?"

"Should we *what*?" I asked.

"Maybe that's not quite the word," Claudia said. "But you know what I mean. Should we make sure we both have the same time, the way they always do in spy movies?"

"Oh, *synchronize*," I said. "Sure." I showed her my watch.

"New Swatch?" asked Claudia. "Cool. When did you buy that?"

"Last time I was in New York. Like it? I was thinking about the blue one, but I thought this one would go with more outfits." Then I caught myself. "What are we doing? Now we only have ten minutes."

Claudia checked her watch. "Right," she answered. "Let's go!" She dashed off toward the cafeteria.

I sprinted in the opposite direction, scanning the halls for green and yellow stripes.

Cary was nowhere in sight.

I checked the science lab, the music room, the auditorium. I even poked my head into the principal's office.

No Cary.

Where could he be? I glanced at my watch again. The minutes were ticking away. If I didn't find him soon, I was going to have to head for math class. How could I sit there answering questions about x and y when I knew the valentine-gram thief was on the loose?

"Thinking deep thoughts?"

I turned to see Alan Gray grinning at me.

"Alan!" I said. "Am I glad to see you."

"You *are*?" he asked, looking shocked.

I laughed. I'm not usually quite so thrilled to come across him. "Yes," I said. "I am."

"Uh, why?" asked Alan suspiciously.

"I thought you might be able to tell me where to find Cary Retlin."

"Oh," he said, sounding strangely relieved. "That's easy. Have you checked the basement?"

"The basement? Why would I check there?"

"Because you want to find Cary, and that's where he hangs out," explained Alan, as if it were the most obvious thing in the world.

"The basement," I repeated, still not believing Alan.

"Yup. Just take those stairs near the library. The ones marked 'No Entry.' "

I knew about those stairs. I'd been down them once before, with my friends. We'd been on the trail of another mystery, and Logan had led us into the basement to search through some old school records. As I remembered, the trip down was dark and gloomy and more than a little scary. I looked at Alan. Should I ask him to come with me?

He grinned at me, that irritating Alan Gray grin.

There was my answer. If it was a choice between going with Alan — who would probably do Dracula laughs and Freddie Krueger imitations the whole way down those dark stairs — and going alone, the verdict was clear.

"Thanks, Alan," I said as I headed off.

"Have a great time," he said. "Don't forget to

write." He was probably grinning again, but I didn't turn around to check. There were seven minutes left, and I didn't have a second to spare.

The trip to the basement was exactly as I'd remembered it. My footsteps echoed as I carefully picked my way down the dimly lit stairs. The heavy steel door at the bottom slammed shut behind me with a crash that made my heart thump. And a dank smell rose to meet me as I felt my way along the darkened hallway, checking for the doors I knew opened off of it.

I opened the first door and peered inside. The room was dark, but when my eyes adjusted I made out a pile of abandoned desks and chairs. There were no humans in sight, and by the look of the thick layer of dust on the desk closest to me, no one had been there for quite some time.

The next door opened into a mop closet that smelled of pine cleaner and floor wax. It was packed with brooms and buckets. There wasn't room for a person as well.

The third door looked familiar. Sure enough, when I peeked inside I saw the room my friends and I had entered during that trip into the "deepest mysteries of SMS," as Logan called the basement.

I looked around at the disorder, which was

lit by two small windows high up in the walls. I saw the same cardboard boxes full of old school records, covered with the same dust and cobwebs. Apparently, Cary was not interested in the ancient history of SMS.

Suddenly, I heard a faraway thump.

Was it one of the custodians?

Was it Cary?

Was it that big steel door, closing and locking this time, trapping me in this dark prison of a basement?

I tried not to panic.

Then I heard another sound, a whooshing noise. It was familiar, somehow. I tried to think where I'd heard it before. Then I remembered. It was the noise our furnace makes at home when it cycles into heating mode. A thump, followed by a whoosh. The furnace room must be nearby.

I left the records room and tried the next door. Sure enough, through the gloom, I could see a network of pipes leading to a huge structure that I knew must be the furnace. I saw the glow of a light coming from behind it. I tiptoed closer and, taking cover behind the furnace, peered around it.

Sitting in an ancient, shabby, overstuffed armchair, reading quietly by the light of a single bare bulb that hung down from a wire, was Cary Retlin. He seemed totally at home.

I swear I didn't make a sound. I wasn't even breathing! But somehow, he knew I was there. "Hi, Stacey," he said, without looking up. "Welcome to my personal library." He shut his book and stood up. He did not seem the least bit surprised to see me.

"What — how — ?" I began.

"I have an arrangement with Mr. Halprin," said Cary. "He understands my need for solitude." He pulled an old packing crate up next to his chair. "Have a seat," he offered politely.

I sat. Somehow, I couldn't think of a thing to say. I stared at his striped shirt, as if I'd been hypnotized.

"Was there something you wanted to ask me?" he prompted.

"Oh, right," I said. Suddenly, it all came flooding back. "Why did you steal the valentine-grams? *That's* what I wanted to ask you." My voice sounded loud to me.

Cary laughed. "I didn't steal them," he said.

"You did," I insisted. "And I have proof." I was still holding the copy, and I showed it to him. "Are those your stripes or not?" I asked.

He just smiled.

Then he began to talk. "Stacey, let me ask you to imagine something," he said, settling back in his chair and putting his fingertips together. "Imagine you're a boy. An eighth-grader at SMS. You make jokes a lot, but that doesn't mean you don't have feelings. It doesn't mean you like it when jokes are made about you." He paused.

"Go on," I said. I heard the distant ring of a bell from upstairs, but I ignored it. Math class seemed a galaxy away.

"Okay, imagine you're this boy," Cary continued. "Valentine's Day is arriving. You like a girl, but you're not sure if she likes you. Maybe you should send her a note to see what she thinks. Nah, too scary. Then you find out your class is sponsoring valentine-grams. Ah! The perfect solution. You write her a valentine-gram. You hand it in." He paused again and looked at me.

I was on the edge of my seat. "Then what?" I asked.

"The next day, you overhear the girl talking to her friends. She's telling them about this great prank. A whole bunch of eighth-graders are going to be sending prank valentines to this boy who annoys them. You."

I gasped.

He nodded and went on. "Imagine you overhear this. How would you feel? You hover near the valentine-gram table, and you see that it's true. People who can't possibly like you are sending you valentine-grams. It's a big joke. And when one of them in particular finds out that you sent them a genuine valentine-gram, it will be an even bigger joke. So, what do you do? Do you sit there and take it? Or do you try to turn the tables? The choice is clear."

"So you did steal the valentine-grams?" I asked.

Cary sighed. "No," he said. "You haven't been listening. And besides, I told you I didn't steal them. I was at the dentist, remember?"

"But you just said you'd try to turn the tables," I said, confused.

"I wasn't talking about myself," said Cary.

Suddenly, I saw that he was telling the truth. I knew he'd been at the dentist. And, as far as I knew, he hadn't sent any valentine-grams. "So it wasn't you?" I said.

Cary smiled and shook his head. "I just helped afterward."

That explained the copied stripes. Again, I knew he wasn't lying. So who was the thief? Who else was still a suspect? Who fit Cary's description? Mentally I ran through the possibilities. Brent? Clarence? Austin? Alan Gray?

Alan Gray!

CHAPTER 14

Thursday

"This was the best Valentine's Day I ever had in my whole life." That's what Archie Rodowsky said to me as he was leaving today. Of course, since he's young, maybe that doesn't mean so much — but I have a feeling the other kids had a good time too. I know I did.

Mary Anne's entry in the BSC notebook went on to describe our Valentine's Day festival in detail, but personally, I think that quote from Archie says it all.

Every single kid there, and every sitter, had an absolutely terrific time that afternoon. Including me. I still hadn't quite wrapped up the valentine-gram mystery, but I had some ideas about what I was going to do next. I had a pretty good hunch that I was closing in on solving the mystery — in time for Valentine's Day no less! Meanwhile, I felt ready to take a couple of hours off and enjoy the fun along with my friends. I hadn't been in on much of the planning, so the event was as much of a surprise to me as it was to our charges. And I think my friends did a fabulous job putting the celebration together.

We arrived a little early at the library, to make sure everything was set.

"Wow!" said Mary Anne. "This place looks gorgeous."

"Ms. Feld wasn't kidding when she said she'd take care of decorations. She really went to town," said Abby.

It was true. The children's room had been transformed. It's always a welcoming place, but today it looked especially cheerful. In the main room Ms. Feld had posted huge pink, red, and white hearts everywhere, each one with a book title inscribed in its center. "Those are all my personal best-loved books," she told us. She'd strung chains of hearts — dozens of them — across the room. She'd set up tables and covered them in red paper. And in the smaller, second room she'd made a special display of books, each one about different kinds of love or friendship, for kids of all ages.

"Oh, look, it's *Shiloh*," said Mal, pulling one book to her chest. "I love this book. It's so, so sad."

"This one's great too," said Claudia, picking up *The Great Gilly Hopkins*.

"And *A Chair for My Mother*. That's one of the best picture books ever," cried Abby.

"Um, girls?" Ms. Feld was smiling. "I'm glad you like the books. But we still have a few things to do before the children arrive."

Kristy, who had just reached for *Romeo and Juliet*, put it back and swung into action. "Right," she said. "Where should we put the food? And which table were you thinking of for crafts?"

With Ms. Feld's direction, we pulled everything together within fifteen minutes — just in time, as it turned out. About two seconds after we'd finished setting up the card-making table, kids began to arrive.

The Braddocks were first, and the Hobart

boys were right behind them. Then Jake and Laurel Kuhn arrived, followed by Carolyn and Marilyn Arnold (identical twins — they're eight years old). The entire Barrett/DeWitt clan showed up: Buddy, Suzi, and Marnie and their stepsiblings — Lindsey, Taylor, Madeleine, and Ryan. Since Ryan and Marnie are only two, Mary Anne offered to take them under her wing.

The Pike kids arrived next, adding considerably to the racket in the room. The triplets were mostly concerned with what time the cupcakes would be served, Claire was eager to start on Valentine making, and Vanessa wanted to know where to set up her free poetry booth.

"I brought my rhyming dictionary," she said, holding it up to show us. "And plenty of nice paper, and my fanciest pens."

"You're writing poems for people?" asked Sara Hill, who'd just arrived with her brother, Norman. "Can you make one for me to send my mom?"

"No problem," said Vanessa. "What's her first name?"

"Michelle," answered Sara.

"Oh, excellent," cried Vanessa. "I don't even need my rhyming dictionary for that. Bell, tell, well . . ."

Kristy herded them into the smaller room and toward the puppet theater, which Ms. Feld

116

had converted into a poetry booth for the day. She could see that Vanessa's booth was going to be majorly popular.

Meanwhile, kids were still arriving. Becca Ramsey and Charlotte Johanssen came, with the Rodowsky boys (Shea, Jackie, and Archie who are nine, seven, and four) right behind them.

"Watch out for that pile of books," Abby called as Jackie walked in.

"What b —" Jackie jumped back as he banged into a carefully arranged display, creating a small avalanche. "I didn't mean to do it," he said quickly, as Abby ran to help him pick up the fallen volumes.

"I know, I know," said Abby, smiling at Jackie fondly. She knows Jackie can't help it. We all do. Our nickname for him is the Walking Disaster. He's a great kid, but make sure you put away the good china if he ever comes to dinner at your house.

Jamie Newton, one of my favorite younger kids, was the last to arrive. "Are we having cupcakes?" he asked as Mary Anne helped him with his jacket.

She laughed and nodded. "Pink ones, with hearts on them," she said. "We'll serve them in a little while. Now, wouldn't you like to come over to my table and make a card for Lucy?" Mary Anne had set up a table for the youngest kids, stocked with blunt scissors, oversized crayons, and plenty of Elmer's glue.

Lucy is Jamie's baby sister, and he's very caught up in his role as big brother. "I'll make her one with kittens on it," he said as he took Mary Anne's hand and allowed himself to be led to a chair. "She loves kittens. Especially gray ones."

"Like my kitten, Tigger?" Mary Anne asked. "Maybe I'll make a card for him. Wouldn't that be silly?"

Jamie giggled as he took a seat between Archie and Marnie.

Meanwhile, at the older-kids' table, Sara was spreading purple glitter thickly over an orange heart. "I'm tired of pink and red," she explained to Abby, who was running the table. "Don't you think this is more creative?"

"Absolutely," said Abby. "I think I'll make a green-and-yellow frog-shaped valentine for my sister. She loves frogs."

"Who doesn't?" asked Adam, who was creating a gory valentine featuring blood and guts.

Abby looked at it and knew it must be for one of his brothers. Only another of the triplets would appreciate such a masterpiece.

At the crafts table, Claudia had her hands full. Literally. Making papier-mâché can be a messy business. But the kids, who included Becca, Charlotte, James, Buddy, Jake, and

Margo, didn't seem to mind. They picked up pieces of paper, dipped them into the bowl of paste Claudia had mixed, and applied them to heart-shaped forms she'd made ahead of time.

As I walked by, I saw Margo and James dip at the same time. Their hands touched — and both of them pulled back. Then they looked at each other and smiled. "What's your favorite color?" Margo asked James.

"Blue," he answered shyly. I saw that famous Hobart blush rising on his cheeks.

"Good," said Margo. "Then that's what color I'll paint this. It's going to be for you."

James gulped. "It is?" he asked. Suddenly he stopped looking shy. Instead, he looked ecstatic. "What's *your* favorite?" he asked Margo.

I didn't stick around to hear her answer. I was on my way to a table in a corner of the smaller room, one we'd set up without telling Ms. Feld what it was for. Mal and Jessi were running it, helping kids create a huge valentine for Ms. Feld and her staff. Every one of our charges loves the library, and this was their chance to let the librarians know how much they are appreciated.

As I walked by, Shea was drawing a dragon on one side of the giant heart while Laurel wrote a note on the other. The valentine was already covered with messages and pictures, and I knew Ms. Feld would love it.

The most touching scene of the Valentine's Day festival was one I didn't witness. Mary Anne told us about it later as we left the library.

"Mathew was so sweet," she said. "He caught me when I was alone, near the end of the festival. I was cleaning up after the little kids while Kristy kept an eye on them. Mathew came up to me in this really hesitant way and handed me a valentine he'd made. 'It's for you,' he said. It was the sweetest card I've ever been given. And as I looked it over, he asked me if I'd be his valentine. Of course I said yes, but I also felt I had to point out that Logan was going to be my valentine too. I was worried that Mathew would be heartbroken, but he seemed happy that I'd said yes, even if he did have to share me. He told me that was fine, and — get this — that all his friends said I was too old for him anyway."

We cracked up. It was a perfect story to end a perfect party. Mathew wasn't the only kid who'd gone home happy that day. Every one of our guests had left with a stomach full of treats, a handful of valentines, and good feelings about each other. What could be better?

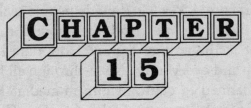

CHAPTER 15

"S-Stacey! What are you doing here?"

Alan's face was white. He was obviously surprised to see me. And I couldn't blame him. After all, it's not often that I stop by Alan Gray's house on a Thursday night.

I'd walked over to the Grays' as soon as the festival was over. I hadn't told my friends where I was going. So far, I was working on a hunch. I wanted to see for myself whether I was right.

I'd been putting the pieces together ever since I'd left Cary's basement lair. My guess was that Alan had stolen the valentine-grams, and that the people he'd pranked were the people who had pranked him. In other words, when he looked over the prank valentine-grams that had been sent to him, he'd recognized Cokie's handwriting, and Jacqui's, and Rose Marie's, and Jim Poirier's. Then he'd done his best to repay the favor by pranking each of them in return, in front of the whole school.

Alan had outdone himself this time. In fact, I thought he'd finally gone too far with one of his practical jokes. He'd made people really angry, including me. And the more I thought about it, the angrier I grew. How dare he put me — and everybody else — through all this?

I planned to confront him immediately and force him to confess. And apologize. Then I'd make him help me figure out how to clean up the mess he'd made of things.

Now I stood facing him, just inside the front door of his house. We were in an entry room with a bench on either side, coathooks along the walls, and a jumble of dog leashes and boots all over the floor. I could hear the sound of a TV coming from the living room. If his parents were home, they were probably watching it. Good. That gave me the chance to speak privately with Alan. I took a seat on one bench and gestured to Alan to sit on the other. He sat.

"Alan, I came to talk about the valentine-grams," I began.

Alan's face grew even whiter. "What — why — ?" he spluttered.

I don't think I've ever seen Alan Gray so off guard. The grin was gone. The devil-may-care attitude was history. And his eyes, which normally gleam mischievously, looked wary.

Suddenly, I remembered some of the things Cary had said that afternoon. I tried to imagine what it might feel like to be Alan. To be a person who plays the fool every day and shrugs it off when people tell him he's a dweeb. I couldn't move past that image of Alan as the SMS Court Jester. It was difficult to think of his having feelings. It was hard to picture his actually liking a girl, and even harder to imagine her liking him back.

But doesn't a jester deserve love as much as the next person?

I felt myself softening. "I want to know if you know anything about the missing valentine-grams," I said.

He didn't say a thing. He just shook his head no.

Alan Gray couldn't even come up with a joke for the occasion. I was stunned.

Now, here's the part I can't quite explain. I'm still not sure what came over me. But, without really knowing why, I decided to give Alan a way out.

"Here's the thing, Alan," I said, leaning toward him just a little and lowering my voice. "I happen to know who stole the valentine-grams. And I know who helped him with the pranks. But right now, my biggest concern isn't punishing those people. My biggest concern is

123

that I want those valentine-grams back. By tomorrow. So that they can be given out, along with the candy, just the way Pete and I planned."

I looked at Alan to make sure he was hearing what I said. He was definitely paying attention.

"If that doesn't happen," I continued, "I just might have to tell Mr. Kingbridge what I know."

I glanced at Alan again. The color was coming back into his face, and he was beginning to look the tiniest bit more like himself. I almost expected him to grin or make some snide remark. If he had, the deal would have been off in a New York minute. I would have hauled him straight into the principal's office first thing in the morning.

But he didn't. He just nodded. "There may be something I can do," he said. Oooh, he was cagey. He hadn't admitted a thing. But I could tell I'd gotten through to him.

"Terrific," I said, jumping to my feet. "Then, I guess I'll see you tomorrow." I was out the door before he'd even stood up.

Friday morning. Valentine's Day had arrived. Would Alan come through? I wasn't sure I could trust him. More than anything, I wanted to be able to deliver those valentine-grams.

I dressed carefully that morning in a pink sweater, white miniskirt, and heart-shaped earrings. And I kept my fingers crossed all the way to school.

Guess what was sitting outside the door of my homeroom when I arrived? A big cardboard box with my name in huge red letters on it. And guess what was inside the box?

The valentine-gram bag.

Yesss! I grabbed the bag, asked my homeroom teacher for permission to leave, and headed out to round up the other eighth-grade officers. Pete was amazed. "Where did you find this?" he demanded, pointing at the bag.

"Outside my homeroom," I answered casually.

"But who put it there? Who took it in the first place?" I think he could tell that I knew more than I was letting on.

I just shrugged. "All I know is that I'm glad to see it back," I said. "Now let's put together these packages and start delivering them!"

We sat down at a table in the library and quickly paired a bag of candy hearts with each valentine-gram. As we worked, I noticed that there wasn't one valentine-gram addressed to Alan — or to Cary, for that matter. I also noticed that several of the valentine-grams looked as if they'd been opened and resealed.

But you know what? By then it didn't matter.

And it didn't matter to anyone else either. By the end of homeroom, we'd managed to fan out and deliver every last valentine-gram. And throughout the rest of the day, I noticed a lot of happy faces in the halls.

My friends and I compared notes at lunchtime, over the cafeteria staff's idea of a perfect Valentine's Day lunch: spaghetti with red sauce, beet salad, and raspberry Jell-O for dessert.

"I saw Cokie and Brent gazing into each other's eyes between second and third period," reported Kristy. "It was one of the grossest sights I've even seen, and that includes the time Boo-Boo threw up a half-digested mouse." (Boo-Boo is Watson's old cat.)

"Oh, ew," said Mary Anne. She pushed her plate away.

"That's what I said when I saw Cokie and Brent," replied Kristy.

"Well, Brian and Rose Marie may not be quite as lovey-dovey as that," Claudia said. She didn't seem fazed by Kristy's gross-out, maybe because she wasn't eating a school lunch. Instead, she was munching on a chocolate-covered granola bar. "But at least they're talking again. I saw them together near his locker. I have a feeling this mess might have brought them closer."

"You know what's funny?" asked Abby. "I saw Sabrina — Miss Perfect Nose herself — holding hands with Jim Poirier."

"And I saw Pete helping Emily Bernstein open her locker when it was stuck," I added.

"That's so sweet!" said Mary Anne. I noticed a valentine-gram from Logan tucked into her notebook and guessed she'd be saving it forever.

"Awww," said Kristy. "A happy ending." She pretended to wipe her eyes.

But she was right. Even Robert and I had been a part of the happy ending. I'd written a quick valentine-gram to him as I was packaging the rest, telling him I hoped we could be friends again. And he'd slipped me a note just before lunch that said he'd like that very much. He'd seemed quite a bit happier the last few days. Maybe having Jacqui out of the picture had had a good effect.

I never did find out which girl Alan had sent the valentine-gram to, but you know what? I wish him well. I hope he can find the courage to let her know he likes her, and I hope he finds out she likes him too.

So, that's the story of my Valentine's Day disaster. And now that I think about it, maybe it wasn't such a disaster after all. Everything had worked out all right in the end.

And I was on my way to enjoy my own Valentine's Day with Ethan.

Still, I thought, leaning back against the headrest as the train pulled into Grand Central Station, I will *never* understand Valentine's Day!

L. GODWIN

About the Author

ANN MATTHEWS MARTIN was born on August 12, 1955. She grew up in Princeton, NJ, with her parents and her younger sister, Jane.

In addition to the Baby-sitters Club books, Ann has written many other books for children. Her favorite is *Ten Kids, No Pets* because she loves big families and she loves animals. Her favorite Baby-sitters Club book is *Kristy's Big Day*.

Ann M. Martin now lives in New York with her cats, Gussie and Woody. Her hobbies are reading, sewing, and needlework — especially making clothes for children.

Look for Mystery #34

MARY ANNE AND THE
HAUNTED BOOKSTORE

I wondered if I should mention the heart-beat. Now that we were in the brightly lit main room with people all around, I wasn't so sure I'd heard anything that unusual. Still, if there was a *drip*, Mr. Cates should know.

"We heard something strange while you were gone," I said.

"Old houses have lots of strange noises, don't they, Gillian?" Mr. Cates said. He kept looking toward the stairs. "You go on up and pick out a game we can play together," he said to her.

" 'Bye, Mary Anne. 'Bye, Mary Anne's boyfriend," Gillian said, running from the room, giggling.

"Claudia told her that's who Logan is," said Mr. Cates, also grinning.

"The noise," I said. "It sounded like . . .

you're going to think I'm crazy, but it sounded like a beating heart." I rushed the last part, then looked to Logan for support.

"It did sort of sound like that," he said.

"It must have been water dripping. There's a place in the basement where water keeps coming in. I'll have some of the guys check it out on Monday," Mr. Cates said. "But Mary Anne, I think a little of our obsession with Poe is starting to rub off on you. Did you know that he wrote a story —"

"—'The Tell-Tale Heart,' " I said, finishing his sentence.

"Exactly," said Mr. Cates. "So you *are* a fan."

"We're studying mysteries in English and I'm doing a project on Poe."

"Good choice!"

Of course, I didn't know what the project was going to be yet. More to the point, I wished that Logan, Mr. Cates, and Ms. Spark would take me a little more seriously.

As we drove away from Poe and Co., I looked back at the house. Dark clouds swirled around it and a flash of lightning split the sky directly above it, lighting the darkened windows for a second. The house seemed almost to throb when the thunder cracked, like a beating heart. I shivered, and not from the chill of the rain.

Read all the books
about **Stacey**
in the Baby-sitters Club series
by Ann M. Martin

#3   *The Truth About Stacey*
      Stacey's different . . . and it's harder on her
      than anyone knows.

#8   *Boy-Crazy Stacey*
      Who needs baby-sitting when there are boys
      around!

#13   *Good-bye Stacey, Good-bye*
      How do you say good-bye to your very best
      friend?

#18   *Stacey's Mistake*
      Stacey has never been so wrong in her life!

#28   *Welcome Back, Stacey!*
      Stacey's moving again . . . back to Stoneybrook!

#35   *Stacey and the Mystery of Stoneybrook*
      Stacey discovers a *haunted house* in Stoneybrook!

#43   *Stacey's Emergency*
      The Baby-sitters are so worried. Something's
      wrong with Stacey.

#51   *Stacey's Ex-Best Friend*
      Is Stacey's old friend Laine super mature or just a
      super snob?

#58   *Stacey's Choice*
      Stacey's parents are both depending on her.
      But how can she choose between them . . . again?

#65   *Stacey's Big Crush*
      Stacey's in LUV . . . with her twenty-two-year-old
      teacher!

#70   *Stacey and the Cheerleaders*
      Stacey becomes part of the "in" crowd when she
      tries out for the cheerleading team.

#76 *Stacey's Lie*
When Stacey tells one lie it turns to another, then
another, then another . . .

#83 *Stacey vs. the BSC*
Is Stacey outgrowing the BSC?

#87 *Stacey and the Bad Girls*
With friends like these, who needs enemies?

#94 *Stacey McGill, Super Sitter*
It's a bird . . . it's a plane . . . it's a super sitter!

#99 *Stacey's Broken Heart*
Who will pick up the pieces?

#105 *Stacey the Math Whiz*
Stacey + Math = Big Excitement!

#111 *Stacey's Secret Friend*
Stacey doesn't want anyone to know that Tess is
her friend.

Mysteries:

#1   *Stacey and the Missing Ring*
Stacey has to find that ring — or business is over
for the Baby-sitters Club!

#10 *Stacey and the Mystery Money*
Who would give Stacey counterfeit money?

#14 *Stacey and the Mystery at the Mall*
Shoplifting, burglaries — mysterious things are
going on at the Washington Mall!

#18 *Stacey and the Mystery at the Empty House*
Stacey enjoys house sitting for the Johanssens —
until she thinks someone's hiding out in the house.

#22 *Stacey and the Haunted Masquerade*
This is one dance that Stacey will *never* forget!

#29 *Stacey and the Fashion Victim*
    Modeling can be deadly.

#33 *Stacey and the Stolen Hearts*
    Stacey has to find the thief before SMS becomes a
    school of broken hearts.

Portrait Collection:

Stacey's Book
    An autobiography of the BSC's big-city girl.

THE BABY-SITTERS CLUB®

by Ann M. Martin

Collect and read these exciting BSC Super Specials, Mysteries, and Super Mysteries along with your favorite Baby-sitters Club books!

BSC Super Specials

❏ BBK44240-6	Baby-sitters on Board! Super Special #1	$3.95
❏ BBK44239-2	Baby-sitters' Summer Vacation Super Special #2	$3.95
❏ BBK43973-1	Baby-sitters' Winter Vacation Super Special #3	$3.95
❏ BBK42493-9	Baby-sitters' Island Adventure Super Special #4	$3.95
❏ BBK43575-2	California Girls! Super Special #5	$3.95
❏ BBK43576-0	New York, New York! Super Special #6	$4.50
❏ BBK44963-X	Snowbound! Super Special #7	$3.95
❏ BBK44962-X	Baby-sitters at Shadow Lake Super Special #8	$3.95
❏ BBK45661-X	Starring The Baby-sitters Club! Super Special #9	$3.95
❏ BBK45674-1	Sea City, Here We Come! Super Special #10	$3.95
❏ BBK47015-9	The Baby-sitters Remember Super Special #11	$3.95
❏ BBK48308-0	Here Come the Bridesmaids! Super Special #12	$3.95
❏ BBK22883-8	Aloha, Baby-sitters! Super Special #13	$4.50
❏ BBK69216-X	BSC in the USA Super Special #14	$4.50

BSC Mysteries

❏ BAI44084-5	#1 Stacey and the Missing Ring	$3.50
❏ BAI44085-3	#2 Beware Dawn!	$3.50
❏ BAI44799-8	#3 Mallory and the Ghost Cat	$3.50
❏ BAI44800-5	#4 Kristy and the Missing Child	$3.50
❏ BAI44801-3	#5 Mary Anne and the Secret in the Attic	$3.50
❏ BAI44961-3	#6 The Mystery at Claudia's House	$3.50
❏ BAI44960-5	#7 Dawn and the Disappearing Dogs	$3.50
❏ BAI44959-1	#8 Jessi and the Jewel Thieves	$3.50
❏ BAI44958-3	#9 Kristy and the Haunted Mansion	$3.50
❏ BAI45696-2	#10 Stacey and the Mystery Money	$3.50
❏ BAI47049-3	#11 Claudia and the Mystery at the Museum	$3.50

More titles ➡

The Baby-sitters Club books continued...

❏ BAI47050-7	#12 Dawn and the Surfer Ghost	$3.50
❏ BAI47051-5	#13 Mary Anne and the Library Mystery	$3.50
❏ BAI47052-3	#14 Stacey and the Mystery at the Mall	$3.50
❏ BAI47053-1	#15 Kristy and the Vampires	$3.50
❏ BAI47054-X	#16 Claudia and the Clue in the Photograph	$3.99
❏ BAI48232-7	#17 Dawn and the Halloween Mystery	$3.50
❏ BAI48233-5	#18 Stacey and the Mystery at the Empty House	$3.50
❏ BAI48234-3	#19 Kristy and the Missing Fortune	$3.50
❏ BAI48309-9	#20 Mary Anne and the Zoo Mystery	$3.50
❏ BAI48310-2	#21 Claudia and the Recipe for Danger	$3.50
❏ BAI22866-8	#22 Stacey and the Haunted Masquerade	$3.50
❏ BAI22867-6	#23 Abby and the Secret Society	$3.99
❏ BAI22868-4	#24 Mary Anne and the Silent Witness	$3.99
❏ BAI22869-2	#25 Kristy and the Middle School Vandal	$3.99
❏ BAI22870-6	#26 Dawn Schafer, Undercover Baby-sitter	$3.99
❏ BA69175-9	#27 Claudia and the Lighthouse Mystery	$3.99
❏ BA69176-7	#28 Abby and the Mystery Baby	$3.99
❏ BA69177-5	#29 Stacey and the Fashion Victim	$3.99
❏ BA69178-3	#30 Kristy and the Mystery Train	$3.99
❏ BA69179-1	#31 Mary Anne and the Music Box Secret	$3.99
❏ BA05972-6	#32 Claudia and the Mystery in the Painting	$3.99

BSC Super Mysteries

❏ BAI48311-0	The Baby-sitters' Haunted House Super Mystery #1	$3.99
❏ BAI22871-4	Baby-sitters Beware Super Mystery #2	$3.99
❏ BAI69180-5	Baby-sitters' Fright Night Super Mystery #3	$4.50

Available wherever you buy books...or use this order form.
Scholastic Inc., P.O. Box 7502, Jefferson City, MO 65102-7502

Please send me the books I have checked above. I am enclosing $ _____
(please add $2.00 to cover shipping and handling). Send check or money order
— no cash or C.O.D.s please.

Name_____Birthdate_____

Address _____

City_____State/Zip_____

Please allow four to six weeks for delivery. Offer good in the U.S. only. Sorry, mail orders are not
available to residents of Canada. Prices subject to change.